Beijing Doll

D1513867

Beijing Doll

A NOVEL

chun sue

TRANSLATED FROM THE CHINESE BY

HOWARD GOLDBLATT

MORAY COUNCIL LIBRARIES & INFO.SERVICES	
2O 12 54 97	
Askews	
⊢	

An *Abacus* Book

First published in Great Britain in 2004 by Abacus

First published in the US in 2004
by Riverhead Books, a division of the Penguin Group

Copyright © Chun Sue 2002
Translation © Howard Goldblatt 2004

The moral right of the author has been asserted.

All rights reserved. No part of this publication may be reproduced, stored in a
retrieval system, or transmitted, in any form or by any means, without the prior
permission in writing of the publisher, nor be otherwise circulated in any form
of binding or cover other than that in which it is published and without a similar
condition including this condition being imposed on the subsequent purchaser.

A CIP catalogue record for this book is available from the British Library.

ISBN 0 349 11679 2

Printed and bound in Great Britain by Clays Ltd, St Ives plc

Abacus
An imprint of
Time Warner Book Group UK
Brettenham House
Lancaster Place
London WC2E 7EN

www.twbg.co.uk

Beijing Doll is my first novel, written three years ago when I was seventeen. Even as I was writing it, I knew that this novel, which records my youth and that of others of my generation, would only reveal its true meaning and value with the passage of time. I truly wanted people to read my novel so they could relate to my youth, its laughter and its tears.

What I hadn't expected was that the publication of *Beijing Doll* would suffer such tremendous difficulty. For over a year, the manuscript made its way to a dozen or more publishers, and all I received was bad news—no one was willing to publish the book. That put me in such a state that I began to think it would never be published. Shen Haobo, my best friend and later the publisher of *Beijing Doll*, comforted and encouraged me to write poetry. It became my new hobby;

it helped me through the period of suffering and confusion before the novel was published.

I was almost nineteen when I finally heard that the book was going to be published. I was thrilled; the news hit me like a bolt of lightning, enabling me to understand many things and to mature quickly. Over the year or so since it was published in Mainland China, I've experienced much that I couldn't ever have imagined. I've received both praise and scorn from readers. Immediately after its publication, the novel caused a huge controversy; reports, critiques, and scandalous rumours flew all over the place. Yet many young people in China wrote to tell me that reading *Beijing Doll* was the most memorable event of their lives. They said it depicted their feelings and reflected the cruelties of youth that we all share: forever angry, never compromising. The novel, they felt, reproduced the painful but true experiences of their secret struggles and confusion, as well as their irreconcilable incompatibility with society, family, and school. It represented the unique characteristics of a new generation in China. These wonderful readers have become my kindred spirits and a source of inspiration. I want to thank them for giving this book a serious reading. It doesn't matter how much resonance they find in it; I'm just happy that they read my writing. Maybe this is how all authors feel.

Present-day Beijing is very different from the Beijing of my childhood; it has grown into a modern, international metropolis. More and more foreigners are coming to China, and in the meantime, the Chinese are becoming more liberated and open. This is a pluralistic age, when people with different views ought to be encouraged. What we need is more distinctive individuality, not conformity. Regrettably, however, there are still a great many people who cannot understand and will not agree with the ideas and behaviour portrayed in *Beijing Doll*, which was banned just a few months after its publication. This was my first novel, in which I invested enormous effort, in which I placed my hopes and dreams, and I was stung by the ban; but also it got me thinking. *Beijing Doll* has already made an indelible impression on Chinese youth, and its influence may, following its translation into foreign languages, prove to be wider still. I hope that people all around the world, the young and the once young, will have a chance to read this book. Although I wrote about the experiences of a Chinese girl, young people everywhere face many of the same issues. I hope to become friends with you.

I'm now twenty years old and am still writing fiction and poetry. Everyone will one day lose their youth, but those days always deserve to be extolled.

I'd like to thank my best friend, Shen Haobo, and Yuan-fang Publishing Company in China. It was you who brought *Beijing Doll* to the eyes of my readers. I also want to thank Ms. Barbara J. Zitwer, my worldwide agent, and Mr. Edmund Cheung in Hong Kong for their enthusiastic promotion of this book outside China. My thanks also go to Ms. Vicki Satlow in Italy and to my many translators—the readers of *Beijing Doll* owe you all a debt of gratitude.

Finally I want to thank all my readers, my parents, other family members, and friends.

Now sit back, settle down, and turn the first page.

CHUN SUE

JULY 2003

some simple introductions
and some loves

This simple list is intended to help you better understand what's in the book. Nothing long-winded for me.

1. My name: I'm Lin Jiafu, a "fine hibiscus", as the name implies. It's what I went by at school. Then I gave myself a new name, Chun Sue. That's what my friends call me, and hearing it makes me happy. So that's my name.

2. West X High: A disgusting school that had one rule: obedience, yes; explanations, no. There was a little white pamphlet called "Educational Guidelines for Student Management". We studied it every day during our first semester, and were required to do everything it said. A ridiculous way to educate. I recall that as soon as I entered high school I had to memorize the following:

"Observe discipline and guard secrets; maintain good, positive work habits; greet others with a smile; be dignified and appropriate in appearance; and be refined and poised in behaviour."

That was followed by two more paragraphs, which I don't feel like putting down here. All this has sparked memories of West X High.

3. Xie Sini: My classmate, my best friend.

4. Rock 'n' roll, punk: My favourite music.

5. B5, A26: Two guidance counsellors from Beijing Normal University I got to know in my third year of middle school.

6. My class monitor, Teacher Wang; third-year monitor, Director Li; and middle-school monitor, Big-Belly Wang.

7. A bunch of poems: Some I wrote, others were by friends. I like poems, they're beautiful.

8. Some guys I used to like.

9. Jelly: A journalist friend of mine. I like his view of "death" from one of his essays.

10. The city of Kaifeng: The air there, the climate, the red lights of its airplanes, and its people.

11. Boiled Water: My friend at The Ark Bookshop, which was once a paradise for young artists.

12. My friends Mary and Ziyu.

13. Beijing University and my fantasies about it.

14. Cui Xiaodi, Wang Yan, Chen Xu, and Du Yuan: Classmates in my first-year high school class.

15. Li Qi and Zhao Ping: Two guys I once loved and hated. The main characters in the first half of the book.

16. Xidan District: I like Xidan in the evening, when it's absolutely captivating, when the night sky is soft and gentle. Lots of people, hip boys and girls, young people, lots of them, like to hang out on the sixth floor of the Huawei Shopping Mall, where the air is saturated with the smell of material stuff.

17. Pangu: a great band that wrote some great songs.

18. G and T: Two guys I loved. The main characters in the second half of the book.

19. Janne: A Finnish boy who loved rock 'n' roll. Tall, squeaky clean, and handsome. Once when I was crying, he said, "You're lost, little girl."

20. Zhang Dongxu: A friend who wrote the book *I'm an Angel, No Lie*. A scribbler.

21. Glass: One of my band's former drummers.

22. Dyeing my hair: I change my hair colour anytime I feel like it. My parents don't approve, but so what. I dye my hair all the time.

23. Parkson Shopping Mall and hanging out there a lot (Long Live Parkson!).

24. Wudaokou: a cool fucking place with lots of colleges and universities nearby.

25. Some poets, musicians, and editors who, at one time or another, entered my consciousness and my life without realizing it and, to some degree, changed them both.

1

birds soaring up from
a thousand peaks

1 | DANCE STEPS OF YOUTH

My third year of middle school was sweet, red, tattered, baffling, and dizzying—loaded with drama. I had lots of friends that year, friends I never saw again after the year ended. They belong to "Middle Three", a year that never grew up.

Dear B5:

Hope this letter finds you well!

Like the Overload lyric, "I once saw a memory from nine angles, I've already forgotten yesterday's news." But I remember our first phone call, when the trees beyond the window were dressed in green, with sunlight raining down like gold. I didn't think I'd be able to write you again, since I'd lost your address, but I found it yesterday when I was cleaning my room, which means we're fated to meet again.

I live in a haze of my own making, on the long road to answers. How are things with you?

Wishing you happiness!

A friend
June 27, 1998

B5 was a guidance counsellor I knew from Beijing Normal University. In the period leading up to our meeting, he had a crush on me and on Xiaojie, another girl my age who lived upstairs in our building. He called us "twin angels". We phoned him every day, sometimes together, which made him laugh. But I stopped liking him once I finally met him in a small park near Beijing Normal. He introduced himself as a "hooligan genius" and said he never refused an offer. "You offering?" We hung around the park for hours. He didn't take me to lunch or walk me home, but I remember the cologne he was wearing and that it drizzled later that day. "You've got pretty eyes," he said, "just the way I like them. Your hands are pretty, too." Later on he asked if I'd seen *Four Weddings and a Funeral*, and I said no, I didn't go to movies much. "That," he said, "was true love, so don't talk to me about love if you haven't seen the movie; you're not qualified to talk about love."

We met one time again. He put his hands on my shoulders, which made me shudder, and I'm sure he noticed. My sense of self-worth vanished when I was with him. I hated myself for not having seen the movies he mentioned, for not having any decent clothes or shoes, for having no class. I totally messed things up with him. But I couldn't stand somebody who sang the words to Luo Dayou's "Love Song 1990" at the same time he was all hung up on desire and money, because that was an endless blasphemy against beauty. That was the last time I saw him.

I met A26 the same way I'd met B5. It was, I think, springtime. Beijing's windy season. The sky was clear. He was a guidance counsellor too and a second-year history major at Beijing University—Beida. We met over the phone. It was the second semester of my third year in middle school, when I had to make the agonizing decision of whether to go on to vocational school or to a regular high school. A vocational school would freeze me out of Beida, but the thought of three more years of lifeless tension nearly killed me. It was such a grim concept, wrapping itself around me every single day, and I figured I'd better decide quick, before it killed me. I hated school, and I hated our class monitor, who was smart but insensitive. But I didn't know what to do, because both options scared me. I knew things like that didn't bother A26, that he could look down on me smugly without batting an eye.

During the busy months leading up to the high school entrance exams, my greatest pleasure was spending half an hour each week on the phone with him. I usually paged him just before dark, when I could look out and see the golden sun and green trees. Our conversations were guarded, with lots of fancy words, like we were living in a fairy tale, where nothing existed but art, order, and beauty. Illusions like that don't stand a chance in the face of reality. He gave me his pager number, which I knew was taboo. For the longest time I didn't even know his name. Everybody has his own space in life, and maybe only during the few hours he worked as a guidance counsellor was he calm and serene, and not distracted.

That's why I didn't phone him too often—I was afraid he might reveal life's limitations and his lack of choices, and all I wanted was some lighthearted conversation. But he was smart enough to know what was going on.

I always said "see ya" before hanging up, but all he'd offer in return was a grunt. "Do you not say 'see ya' out of habit? Or is there some other reason?" I asked him. There was a pause before he said, "That's weird. Nobody's ever noticed that before. I don't say see ya, because my understanding of the term is I'll never see ya again."

Because of him, I signed up in April for an early entrance exam for the liberal arts section at Number Two Beijing Normal High. I didn't pass. My friend Xiaoshui and I took it together. She passed, I didn't. I sucked at maths. Beijing Normal High was only a block from the university, where there was a wooded area with beautiful Chinese roses. Wearing a white skirt, I strolled around the Beijing Normal campus that day, telling myself that these were places where Blue-grass, which was what I called A26, had walked and lived, and that made me warm and melancholy at the same time.

I started paging him more often. He was the bright spot in my third year of middle school, a sort of consolation; I didn't want to lose him, couldn't go without hearing his voice. He'd phone me from the library and hang up after a minute or so.

He kept saying he wanted to meet, and I kept putting it off. Then one day I agreed. I just about went crazy trying to find something to wear. I hadn't bought a single thing all that year in Middle Three, and I'd put on weight. My self-confidence was a mess. I was afraid he wouldn't like what he saw. I went to borrow some clothes from a neighbour, and tried on everything—white skirt, patterned skirt, blue jeans, black jeans—until I started getting dizzy, and I didn't leave for our 7:30 meeting until 7:20. I was wearing brown pants that weren't really me, but by the time I tried them on, my head was already spininng. I took the subway to Jishuitan, but didn't dare approach any of the exits; instead I looked at each one from a distance, then lowered my head and listened to a Xu Wei song. At ten that night I called his house. His dad answered and said he'd already gone to bed.

The next day I began dialling his pager number, which I knew by heart. I wanted to tell him I loved him, didn't want him to leave me, didn't want him to be mad at me. I was just a girl who liked him but couldn't say the words. I wanted to satisfy all his demands on me—if he had any, that is. But I got no answer. All I did that day, from morning to night, was dial his pager number, then cry when no call came. I was a basket case because of him, and I really wanted to explain why I hadn't shown up that day and tell him everything that was on my mind. I heard the phone ring several times, but each time I ran to answer, I discovered it was all in my head, that the phone hadn't rung at all. I dug out his address and wrote him a letter, even enclosing photos of me. I hardly ever had my picture taken; except for those from my childhood, I only had a few pictures of me, and I sent him every one. Later on I learned he never got the letter, that it was lost in the mail. Like all important things, I have no idea what became of it.

A week later, Bluegrass reappeared. He called without warning. It felt kind of strange to hear his voice this time. In a tone that had lost its familiarity, he asked me what I'd done on Friday.

"Went to school."

"Wrong. What if I said I was mad at you for not showing up the other day? . . ."

"I did go."

"Maybe you did, which makes me just as mad. I kept calling, all day long, but you weren't home. If you hadn't been home today to take my call, then you could have just kissed our whole thing good-bye."

I said I'd moved and had only today brought the phone over from the old place. He asked me if I loved him, and I didn't know what to say. Sure, I thought I loved him, but it never dawned on me to actually say so. That freaked me out.

"Ask me that again, okay?"

That stopped him for a second. "Do you love me?"

"With feeling."

"Do you love me?"

"Yes, I love you."

"Say that again, okay?"

"Yes, I love you."

"With feeling."

"I love you. My love for you feels like birds soaring up from a thousand peaks."

Weakly he said, "Don't love me."

Then it was the entrance exams, and my middle school years came to an end. A chaotic sensitive innocent age came to an end, and everything belonging to that age ceased to exist. I discovered that, in Bluegrass's presence, I found myself slipping away. That hurt like hell. I could barely conjure up the comfortable, pleasant, free and easy feeling associated with a normal relationship. But I don't mind saying that my time with him had its share of happiness. Caught up in this internal struggle, filled with contradictions, I felt like I was drowning a little at a time. I couldn't control my emotions. Maybe, since he was a guidance counsellor, I was just one of his "patients". He never treated me as a friend. Could that be it?

I phoned him to say good-bye.

The entrance exams ended; I wrote to several friends of that period, then burned my diary and set out to start my life all over again. I doubt there are many people who ended up hating Middle Three as much as I did. In a word, it was one shitty year. I thought graduation day would never come, and the last thing I wanted was to beat up on myself with a rehash of all that had happened. Those days were over, and I had no desire to bring them back.

A secret agent or a hired assassin should have no past and no future, so that they can disappear in an instant. The killer Li Ming in the movie *Fallen Angel* kept his childhood classmate, and that was his undoing. Although I'm neither a secret agent nor a hired assassin, those are two of my favourite occupations, because they're all tied up with mystery, intelligence, and the thin line between life and death. I can't deny that I get a kick out of danger.

I failed the high school entrance exam. That's because I listed Number Two Beijing Normal High as my first choice, a classic example of aiming too high. It wouldn't have made a difference anyway, since my dreams were surely beyond my reach and inside I was a mess. If I'd had the luck to step once more onto the grounds of Number Two Beijing Normal High, how would I have felt? I'd probably have thought back to how oddly happy and proud I'd been the time I took the early liberal arts exam. It was springtime, with Chinese roses sending their fragrance across the campus; there were trees, grassy lawns . . . a sense of time repeating itself.

I was accepted into a vocational school near the Summer Palace. A five-minute bike ride from Beida's western gate. Also not far from the Haidian Book City. My main reason for choosing that school was its proximity to Beida, which I was obsessed with at the time. The other reason was that the school had the word "Xi" [West] in it, and I liked that there used to be a poet at Beida called Xi Chuan [West River]. How was I to know I'd escaped from the wolf's lair only to wind up in the tiger's den?

2 | MAKING A FRIEND

There was a letter waiting for me downstairs in the janitor's room. I saw by the postmark that it had been mailed in the city and was addressed to "Chun Sue". That was strange— who'd be calling me that? I'd only used that name a few times when I'd conducted interviews for music magazines, and none had included my address. Then it hit me: While I was bored out of my mind in Middle Three, I'd sent a "Seeking Friends" notice to a music magazine, and they must have published it. That had been nearly a year ago. I opened the envelope, and that's what it was. He said he'd spotted my notice and wanted to see if we could be friends. He said his name was Li Qi and that he was an art student in Beijing. He invited me to come to see him when I had some free time. At the bottom he added a serious note, that he hoped I'd become a "model Young Pioneer".

I thought back to the notice I'd sent in. I think I said I liked U2, Xu Wei, Nirvana, Kafka, and computers. At the time, mentioning Nirvana showed you were hip. Not impossibly passé, like now.

Excited, I wrote a reply and mailed it, but his next letter took its own sweet time getting to me. It came about two weeks later. He said he'd just returned from a trip back home to Shandong.

Then one day the phone rang, and the person on the other end asked for Chun Sue.

"That's me," I said.

"Oh . . ." He sounded surprised. "I thought you'd be a guy!"

We settled on a day for me to go to see him.

"I won't be late," I added, even though I knew I probably would be.

It was a foggy Saturday morning when I took the subway to Jishuitan. He'd said he was a student at the Lu Xun Art Academy, so we'd agreed to meet at the front gate. I looked at my watch and saw I was already a good ten minutes late, so I walked up feeling goofy and guilty at the same time. Someone was leaning against a tree at the academy entrance watching me as I crossed the street, so I sped up a bit. "I'm Chun Sue," I said. He stuck out his hand, and we shook hands. Then we turned and started walking. It was kind of awkward. He was nothing like I'd imagined. His hair was sort of long, and he looked like a poet, down on his luck. He had on a leather jacket, his skin was very light, and he was pretty skinny. I figured I was nothing like he'd imagined either.

He led me down a tiny lane opposite a music and video shop not far from his school. He lived in a rented room in a small but typical Beijing quadrangular compound, not the sort of place I'm used to. I much prefer tall buildings and bright, sunny places.

I stepped cautiously into his room. It was barely big enough to hold a bed. One wall was practically filled with audiotapes. I sat on the edge of his bed, and we just talked for a while about this and that. He looked nervous. The room was dark, dank, and unheated. Li Qi got up and poured me a glass of water, which I drank. A few rays of sunlight came in through the window. Then an ordinary, unspectacular morning started feeling wrong, the mood and situation were reeling off course, and I could sense that things had already moved beyond my control. Or maybe I just wanted to see what could happen, see if there were mortal consequences. Like I said, I love playing with danger. At the time I had no idea that something was bearing down on me, and it all happened so fast, too fast for me to stop it. It was like I'd suddenly been thrust into a nature painting, and I was out of tune with my surroundings. I think Li said something, but since he was facing the wall, I could only make out a bit about how people should listen to their desires, be true to something or other, then silence. I forget what I said or did then, but I must have done something to arouse him, because he threw his arms around me. He took off my shoes. I was wearing white stockings with embroidery up the sides. We stayed like that, with our arms around each other, for a while, before Li stood up and said triumphantly, "Stay there while I go and bring in the quilt I hung out in the sun." He walked out and quickly returned with it. We lay down on the bed and started kissing. None of it seemed quite real.

* * *

"Blood," I said to him.

"Oh." He wiped it clean with some toilet paper, which he tossed on the floor. "How old are you?" he asked, as if it had just then occurred to him.

"Sixteen," I lied. Without saying a word, he lit a cigarette. He looked spent.

"Do you have a girlfriend?" I asked casually.

"Yes."

That blew me away.

He told me the girl's name was Cai Yun. From then on, he never mentioned her without calling her his girlfriend. Like "my girlfriend this" and "my girlfriend that".

I was dizzy and clearheaded at the same time. I didn't know how to describe what I was thinking, but when I cleared my throat, I realized there was no need to even try. Li had no real desire to be with me; it never dawned on him that I might be someone with thoughts of her own and a need to express them.

At noon we went out for some lunch, steamed dumplings and wontons at a little café. I don't know if it was a habit he'd formed over the years, but he hardly ate anything.

That's pretty much how the day went. We went back to his place after eating, with me hanging naturally on his arm, feeling that since we'd become what we were, it was the thing to do. But he frowned slightly, so I jerked my arm back, embarrassed. And sort of at a loss. "Did you know," I said to break the ice, "that I memorized the poem 'Everlasting Sorrow'? I've forgotten some of the lines, but I still remember most of them. . . ."

On my way back to the subway station, I walked down early evening streets, the fading sunlight sprinkling down on my face and the tips of my hair. A vendor squatting in the subway entrance had a big bucket of cut flowers, including my favourites—roses and lilies. It was late October, the last gasp of freshness and splendour in Beijing.

He called after I got home. I can't recall what he said, but the anxiety in his voice told me he was worried I'd take him to court, and he'd end up in jail. Right.

3 | LI QI

He told me his name was Li Qi. From Shandong. Original name, Li Xiaolai. Studied at the Lu Xun Art Academy. Loved literature, painting, music, once organized a band called Appendix (meaning it was redundant, something useless), which performed somewhere or other.

I know, that reads like a missing persons notice. But I think it's best to introduce him as factually as possible.

He had a girlfriend, from the same village; he showed me her picture once, nothing special, but someone who seemed to know how to live. He also showed me pictures of the two of them, both smiling, with Li Qi appearing almost childlike, the sweet look of a spoiled kid with his nanny, making his girlfriend look pretty serious. One of the pictures had been partially burned, which I could see from the grey scars; the burned portion must have represented some tragedy or conflict. He said that the romance had died. He didn't say he loved her, he just said, "What can I do? I can't leave her," because she'd already attempted suicide more than once, and told him that if he got involved with anybody else or tried to leave her, she'd kill herself. His tone of voice betrayed a sense of fatalism. To me, her neediness was degrading, but he actually called the failed process of needing one another and struggling with the idea of leaving "love". How could someone like me, a perfectionist, be content with that?

Li Qi often wrote poetry too. That was the winter of 1998, before he'd made a name for himself, and financially he was in bad shape. For lunch, most of the time he asked his kindly old team monitor to get him a bowl of rice, then he shared the other fellow's vegetables and meat. That's all he could do. He was broke. Which is why he also occasionally considered suicide. He once told me he'd written some poems and wanted to read them to me. He was really proud of one of them. It went something like, "A bird flew over and landed on my finger . . ." Then something something something, until the last line, that went, "Excitement came when the third bird flew over." (Ha, I'm not sure if I got it right after all this time.) He asked me how I liked it, but the weird part is, I never much cared for his poems. To this day, I have no idea what attracted me to him. Maybe nothing. But every day was like a dream.

* * *

On Sunday night I told my friend Jelly I wanted to see him. At the time he was an editor for *The Music Life*. We agreed to meet in front of his place at Fuchengmen, and I arrived in the middle of a gorgeous sunset, when the air smelled fresh and clean. Jelly was waiting for me, leaning against a railing around his compound. He waved, obviously happy to see me. I was wearing casual pink clothes, he had on a grey jacket and blue jeans. His hair was cut really short, like an innocent teenager. I ran over, and the two of us started walking toward Tiananmen Square. To us that was a sacred place. The road-side soft-drink stands were already lit up, the sky was an almost transparent blue, and I was an emotional wreck. What had happened between Li Qi and me the night before kept replaying in my head, and I was wrenched by a mood I couldn't understand, let alone describe. It was so bad I could hardly breathe, and couldn't think straight.

I made up my mind. "Jelly, there's something I have to tell you."

Jelly looked puzzled. My face was ashen as I told him exactly what Li Qi and I had done, from start to finish. He was as surprised as I expected, and he fidgeted as he heard me out. Then he told me he was still a virgin. Maybe it was my openness that sparked his desire to talk. He told me he'd fallen for a girl, a real pretty sixteen- or seventeen-year-old nurse, and she liked him, though he hadn't told her how he felt. "She's so young," he said, keeping his head down. "I don't want to do anything to hurt her." By then we were walking down Chang'an Avenue, and I realized that talking to Jelly had done nothing to make me feel better. I knew that what I really wanted was to talk to Li Qi, that my heart felt empty. Obviously, what had happened was a big deal to me, but there was no one to hear what I wanted to say.

I went to school on Monday as usual. The same road as always, but the atmosphere felt different. There was a heaviness in my heart, while something uncontrollable was messing with my head. Li's name had forced its way into my consciousness, and it all happened so fast I didn't have time to adjust. Something deep down kept me on pins and needles, I couldn't concentrate on anything that was going on around me, and I was incapable of putting what had happened out of my mind, which was filled with crazy, confused fantasies. And they got worse. I was scared that the emotions and confused state of mind that Bluegrass had aroused in me during Middle Three would resurface. But the deepest impression I had was the sort of feeling you get from smoking pot. Polar lights, blinding terror. I was really freaking out.

*　*　*

I went to see Li Qi again on Saturday. While we lay in bed, he told me an old girlfriend had come to see him the day before.

"Was it Cai Yun?" I asked nervously.

"No, somebody else." He lit a cigarette, took a drag, and continued: "She came looking for me at school. She called me Little Lai. Remember, I told you I used to be called Little Lai Li? She came at noon, when I was out, so the class monitor told her where I lived. She came to see me that night."

I listened without saying a word. He glanced over at me. "This place isn't heated, as you know, so I decided to take her over to the class monitor's place for the night."

"What did he do?"

"He spent the night here."

"Did you two make love?"

"Of course." He seemed genuinely surprised that I'd even ask.

"How come?"

"She made a special trip to see me, the poor thing, so I had to make her feel good. . . ."

"You figured that was the way to make her feel good?"

"Well, I didn't want her to be unhappy."

"Then you . . ."

"She'd made a special trip to see me, coming all that way, asking around to see where I live. I don't know what she's doing these days . . . maybe she's a whore."

While we were lying in bed, Li lit another cigarette, a sad look on his face. I was wrapped up in my own thoughts.

"Do you love me?" I asked him.

"No," he said without hesitation. "I don't love anybody."

That brought tears to my eyes. He was so direct, so honest, but it wasn't what I wanted to hear. The table lamp gave off a muted yellow light. The hard covers of the art albums and thick philosophy books Li had stacked on my side of the bed dug into me, but I forced myself not to move as I lay there crying, not saying a word.

"I'm sorry," Li Qi said.

"I don't need your apologies." I tried to stop crying, but it didn't help, and I just lay there wiping away the stream of heartbroken tears.

* * *

The next night, while I was talking with my good friend Ziyu, I decided to ask him if he'd go with me to see someone. I didn't want to go alone. He baulked, and I think he might have had a hint what it was all about. "Okay," he said after a moment. "How do we get there?"

"Subway to Jishuitan."

We didn't talk on our way to the subway station. Ziyu was someone who knew what questions not to ask. We kept a comfortable distance in our relationship, clean and clear, like pure water, though from time to time I honestly wished he'd ask me something personal.

When we left the subway station, I told Ziyu that if Li Qi was home, he didn't have to stick around. If Li wasn't home, then he and I could head back together.

He said okay.

He always said okay, no matter what I asked. That included unreasonable requests. Like I said, he was a good friend.

I told him to wait outside Li's compound. "If I'm not back in five minutes, you can leave."

"Here, this is for you." Ziyu handed me a folded slip of paper. He didn't look any different than usual, steady and detached, except for a hint of agitation or maybe even distress on his face. "Don't open it yet, wait till after I leave," he said, his breath quickening. I saw his toothy smile in the dark.

"Okay." I took the slip of paper, which was damp from his sweaty hand. "Wait five minutes. If I'm not back, you can take off."

I walked into the compound. There was a lock on Li Qi's door. Disappointment and anxiety washed over me.

Ziyu was surprised to see me walk out. "What's wrong? Not home?"

"No, and that's strange," I said. "Where do you think he might have gone?"

"Why don't we wait here a while?" Ziyu suggested.

"Sounds okay to me." I was still clutching the unopened slip of paper as I leaned against the wall. Thin splinters of orange light from streetlamps slipped through the shadowy treetops. After about a quarter of an hour, we spotted the silhouettes of two people coming our way.

"Is that you, Chun Sue?" Li Qi's old class monitor spotted us. I walked over. "Hi."

"What are you doing here?" Li asked me.

"I just felt like coming to see you."

"Well, I'll be going," Ziyu said, glancing at me as he walked off. His white shirt glowed in the lamplight.

The rest of us went into Li's room. I made a point of breathing deeply to take in the room's smell. It had only been a day since I'd last seen him, but at that moment I thought I could never leave him, not for anything.

After a while, Li's class monitor said good-bye, leaving the two of us sitting across from one another.

"What are you doing here?" he asked again.

I smiled, but didn't answer.

By the time I'd taken my practised position beneath him, naked, I had again come to the realization that we ought to bring this to an end.

Exhausted, we fell asleep. At sometime around eleven, he woke me. "Chun Sue, I'm sorry, but you'd better go now." I climbed out of bed and got dressed, and he walked me to the subway station. He waved good-bye on the upper deck, I waved back, then he turned and walked off.

But when I went up to the ticket window, the clerk told me the last train had left only a minute before. "Shit!" I cursed under my breath, before taking off after Li Qi. He was walking slowly, carrying a plastic bag with two apples he'd just bought. I quickly caught up with him. "Hey!" I thumped him on the shoulder.

"I thought you left." I saw he was pleasantly surprised.

"Missed the last train," I said.

"Now what? You've got school tomorrow. I'll take you home on my bike." He smiled.

"That's okay." Letting him give me a ride would mean I owed him, and I didn't want that. This was better, no one owed anyone anything.

So we went back to his place to eat the apples. While he was paring them with a knife, he said sternly, "Coming home with me like this puts a dent in my finances."

"You mean the apple?"

"Yeah." He didn't appear to be joking.

"Bullshit! You don't mean that," I said cheerfully.

Before going to sleep, I opened the grimy slip of paper Ziyu had given me. He'd written the following in his delicate, cautious handwriting: "Tragedy lurks tonight. On the way home, there'll be an explosion on the subway, and I'll be the only survivor. Ha ha, good-bye forever!"

I slept badly that night. We didn't make love a second time. In fact, we barely touched, sleeping as far away from each other as the bed would allow. Mutual disgust. We'd lost interest in each other. For me, there was also the terrifying reality that I'd stayed out all night, plus the pressure of getting up early the next day for school, and that worried me. I'd been yearning to spend a night with Li Qi, but now that I actually had the chance, my passion for him had vanished. How come all of a sudden I didn't feel the tiniest bit of love for him? Weird. I lay there having all these crazy thoughts. Then there was Ziyu—he had to know what was going on with me and Li Qi, and I wondered how he felt about that. Sad? Worried about me? Were we really only everyday "good" friends? And what was I going to say to my mother the next day? Last night I . . . I kept breathing faster and faster, my mouth was dry, and I tossed and turned all night. No dreams. It was one of the longest nights of my life.

I took the first subway the next morning and went straight home. When my mother heard the key in the lock, she ran into the living room just in time to see me walk in, cutting a sorry figure, with my dirty face and uncombed hair. It was the first time I'd ever stayed out all night, and she was fit to be tied, her pent-up anger exploding in a stream of curses.

"You can stop now, I've heard enough," I pleaded. "I'm exhausted, and I need twenty RMB for a taxi to go to school. I'm almost late." I stuck out my hand.

My mother froze for a moment, then took twenty RMB out of her purse and handed it to me before heading back to bed, cursing me the whole way. I must have been a big disappointment to her, but I was too tired to care.

4 | SECLUSION

> My heart is broken, but I'm out of glue.
> —Xiaoshui

It snowed on Saturday, when Li Qi and I were at his place. I'd arrived at eight or nine in the morning, before it was really light out, and he was in bed, waiting for me. I slipped under the warm, filthy comforter to cover my ice-cold body. As always, he wrapped his arms around me, like he was afraid I'd run away or simply vanish. We were never able to control our passion or our desires. The room was pitch black, so I sneaked a look out the window at the gloomy grey sky. When I felt thirsty, I picked up his mug and was about to drink, but he grabbed it, dumped the cold water onto the floor, and refilled the mug with hot water. He said it's a bad idea to drink cold water when you're like this.

After lunch, I went with him to see his old class monitor, but the door was locked, so after standing in the snow for a few minutes, we left. I asked him to tell me the difference between punk and grunge. Every week Li lent me tapes by bands like Green Day, Blur, R.E.M., The Pixies, and Sonic Youth. I'd return them when we got together the following Saturday. He dug his fingernail into one of the bricks on the wall, stammering to explain the difference. Finally he said he wasn't sure either.

We tromped through the snow back to his place. Snow covered the branches of trees, and before long it covered my jacket too. The ground was quickly becoming a soggy, depressing grey. "Why don't we just walk a while," I suggested. No response. We walked up to a music and video shop opposite his lane, where pirated copies of Hong Kong rock 'n' roll tapes went for five RMB apiece. I didn't even have five RMB. After rummaging through the piles of tapes without either of us intending to buy any, I said, "Let's go home."

"Didn't you say you wanted to walk for a while?"

"Forget it," I said. "I don't feel like it."

Back in his room we climbed into bed to talk and read. He

turned philosophical. He told me to work hard at my studies, but the very mention of school pissed me off, even though I understood what he was saying. It's just that the future was a mystery to me; I had no idea how things would turn out. Li Qi wanted me to live my life right and not follow in his foot-steps. He didn't want me to wind up like him someday, alone, away from home, broke, jobless, no career, no love. Existing on handouts. He said I should try to get into a college, then find a good job. It was obvious he wasn't enjoying life, and that staying in Beijing kept him feeling unsettled and help-less. But I wasn't like that. I wanted a happy, meaningful life. Still, I hadn't studied at all during my third year in middle school, not maths, not chemistry, not physics. Maybe my hormones were acting up. I just wrote stories, and our class monitor, who thought I was crazy, would've killed me if he could have. Now I was enrolled in another tyrannical school, where I was afraid of the teachers, the principal, and all the administrators. Deeply introverted, I found it hard to express myself, even harder to socialize. And I was too trusting.

So lonely. But that's life.

From time to time, I let Li Qi read some essays and poems I'd written, but he thought that reading them was beneath him. Maybe to him I was just a kid. I never really meant any-thing to him. Afterward he told someone that at the time I made myself up like a little boy.

Li's philosophy pretty much went: "God didn't create life out of kindness, that's for sure, and bestowing intelligence on humans was an act of malice. Everything's absurd. Anyone seeking meaning in life is uncommonly sick, and God is uncommonly fucking evil. . . ." His favourite words were things like glorious, absurd, and useless power. His gloomy eccentricity closed out the possibility of any real emotional involvement with anyone, especially love. Even so, during that time, my heart was completely tied to him. I didn't call him my boyfriend, because he wasn't, but when he talked about Cai Yun and kept referring to her as his girlfriend, it was sheer torture. But that didn't stop me from wanting to see him as often as possible, from wanting to spend time with him. I went to his place every Saturday, taking all sorts of snacks and food with me—preserved plums, crackers, gum, stuff like that. He'd tell me to save the money and stop bringing him things. But that didn't keep him from happily scarfing everything down. I even entertained the thought of buying him new curtains, sheets, and pillowcases. Day in and day out, I thought up things to do for him, which made me unbelievably happy and unbelievably muddled.

At first the silver-haired lady with bound feet—his landlady—watched us like a hawk whenever we went out to eat. But after a while, the sight of us no longer alarmed her, and she assumed that I was Li Qi's live-in girlfriend. At first she'd treated him like a dumb kid, but now she didn't dare. He joked that from now on, when I came over, I should stick a piece of paper on the door, saying, "Deliberations in session. Please do not disturb." He thought that was really funny, and actually took out a sheet of paper, sort of goofy-like, scribbled some words on it in big letters, and stuck it on the door. "That'll do it. No one will bother us now," he said. Usually we had steamed dumplings or rice porridge for lunch or dinner; sometimes we opted for noodles or wontons. That's how we spent every Saturday, and I never tired of it.

After we got together, I continued sending him letters, even though he stopped writing to me. Sometimes in typing class, on an impulse, I'd knock out a letter on a manual typewriter in horrible English. To me that was romantic, but it probably just proved to him how dumb I was.

5 | PAGODA REFLECTED IN A LAKE

Over time, I've forgotten exactly what Li Qi wrote in his last letter to me. All I remember is how cold my hands and feet were when it arrived. I couldn't believe he'd dump me so abruptly. He said he'd gone to Guangzhou to see his "girlfriend", and was going to stay through New Year's. The prick had actually encouraged me to "study hard". Uncontrollable rage. I was pulverized. I really didn't love him, I'd even thought of breaking it off, since being with him had only brought conflicting feelings and unhappiness. But I couldn't stand the thought of not having him. Stubbornly, he'd become a part of my life. Now, without a word to me, he'd gone to Guangzhou to be with another woman, leaving behind only a letter, abandoning me in Beijing. I couldn't stand that. An uncontrollable anxiety gripped me, and I spent every day crying, so listless I couldn't get anything done. In his letter he'd said he left the CDs he'd borrowed with his landlady, and I could pick them up on Saturday or Sunday. A quick check of dates showed he was already in Guangzhou.

Saturday I went over to pick up my CDs. If I hadn't borrowed them from a friend, I'd never have bothered. I knocked at his landlady's door; she opened it and handed me a plastic bag. Her expression revealed nothing, but I was sure she knew that Li had dumped me before going to Guangzhou to be with his girlfriend. She had to know. And she had to be silently mocking me for proving exactly what she'd thought all along, that there was no way Li could be in love with me. How could he have given a damn about me? Mortified, I took the plastic bag, thanked her, and walked out the gate, thinking of the band PK14's lyrics—

So young, a moist heart, so young, an empty heart, a seemingly endless winter, a raw winter, so young, a moist heart, I sit at the window and watch you wither, I am without hope, my heart is moist, I am waiting for your arrival, waiting for you to grab me, waiting for your arrival, my heart is moist, I am without hope, so young.

I was just as listless at school, and I kept failing my computer class tests. Our class monitor was about to give up on me, but I didn't have it in me to tell her what was wrong.

* * *

I went to see Jelly again. Whenever I was down, he'd listen to me bitch and complain about being so indecisive. He said I was a girl with a problem, someone who let herself get hurt because she was too sensitive and insecure. We went to Beida, where the ground was covered with leaves from the gingko trees, a carpet of yellow that shifted beautifully in the wind. So happy. We strolled along the edge of Weiming Lake. The lake was so beautiful. People who lived by the pagoda reflected in the lake were so happy. "People fishing over there," Jelly blurted out.

"Really?" I'd just passed a sign that said "Man-made lake. No fishing or swimming." The words were barely out of my mouth when I spotted some people squatting on the shore fishing. One had just caught a little fish and was celebrating. In that moment, the lustre of the pagoda in the lake seemed to fade. Jelly said I took an extreme view of everything.

We sat on a bench, and I told him that Li and I had broken up.

"Broke up? You were never together, so how could you break up?" he said with a sneer. He said I never did know my place, which definitely was not in Li's heart.

I sat there gaping. Li and I had never been a couple, so I had no right to talk about breaking up. But then why was I so miserable? God, what an idiot I was. I shook my head, but held my tongue.

We started talking about dying. Jelly said his greatest hope was that someone would put a bullet in his head. Jumping off a building was too painful, he said, which immediately drove away the thought that, if I ever decided to kill myself, I'd jump out a window. I wanted to know the least painful and most respectable kind of death. A tough question, apparently with no good answer. Then we began talking about Bluegrass. He asked if I still had feelings for him, since it seemed like he was still on my mind.

"Of course!" I said. "I think I still remember his phone number: 6421 XXXX, but I could be wrong. Maybe I'll give it a try after we leave Beida."

As soon as I'd said it Jelly whipped out his mobile phone. "Try it now," he said. I froze for a moment. I'd backed myself into a corner. Might as well try. The call went through. His father said that Bluegrass wasn't home, that he'd gone to school. That was a relief. As I put away the phone, I had a weird feeling: Bluegrass seemed more like a fairy tale from a hundred years ago, yet I remembered his name and his phone number. It was like suddenly being carried back in time, amazing. But I didn't want to call him again. Back in Middle Three I'd had no confidence that I was his intellectual equal, and I realized that nothing had changed.

6 | BORN AT THE RIGHT TIME

Jelly told me he lived with his mother.

He had a computer in his room, which was surprising back then. He slept on a very low bed, said he had a problem with heights. His walls were covered with photographs, two of which were enlargements: one of him at the age of twenty-four, and another of his kid sister at nineteen. Collections of poetry by Gu Cheng, Bei Dao, and Xi Chuan, and lots of other books that made me envious, lined his bookshelf.

I went to see him one afternoon, and a friend of his was there. He was short, very slight, and dark-skinned. Jelly called him Comrade Wang. The three of us were chatting by the gate when a guy pushing a bicycle came up to Comrade Wang and whispered, "Got any white?" Comrade Wang didn't know what he was talking about.

"What?"

"Powder!"

"No . . ." Comrade Wang was scared half to death. And for good reason, since a cop walked up right after the guy left.

"Fuck! Do I look like someone who snorts coke?" Jelly and I laughed at him.

Back in the room, Comrade Wang started talking shit about "punks", saying they were a bunch of nihilists, and much too cocky. Jelly and I were so mad all we could do was laugh. Then he called me his "little punky friend". His preachy tone pissed me off. "I'm not talking to you anymore," I said. "I make it a rule never to talk to people I can't get along with." They both laughed.

After a while, a girl phoned Jelly and asked him to go to Tiananmen Square. He wanted to beg off, but wasn't sure how. After he hung up, Comrade Wang asked him who it was. "Some girl from the Beijing Film Academy," he said. "Hell, let's go to Tiananmen."

So we went. The square was packed, and cynical Comrade Wang kept asking why all those assholes weren't home where they belonged. Then he started teasing me. No matter what I said, he disagreed. Like I said I planned to buy a mobile phone, and he said, "Little Punky, that stuff's out of the question for us punks. We're lucky to have pagers." Eventually, we wound up in a bar, where they drank beer and I had orange juice. I don't know how long we stayed there, since I wouldn't let them tell me the time. I didn't want to think about going home. They sang karaoke; I didn't. Jelly asked why. I said I was embarrassed to, maybe some other time.

"When?" he pressed me.

"Some other time."

Comrade Wang was always a beat behind whatever song he was singing. And Jelly did an off-key rendition of "Greenhouse Girl". They drank a lot. It had to be after two in the morning when we finally left, though I can't say for sure.

Outside in the cold wind, Jelly pissed me off by asking, "When are you going home?" I ignored him, but was hurt. He could probably tell. We grabbed a taxi and drove down the nearly deserted avenue. I rested my head on Jelly's shoulder and hugged his arm. My hands were freezing. My thoughts were all over the place.

"There are things I don't want to talk about," I said.

"Then don't say anything," he said to put me at ease.

Finally, the taxi stopped. The time had both flown by and dragged on. The thought of going home terrified me at that hour, because my parents would probably kill me. Without a word, Jelly put his arm around me. Finally he said, "We'll worry about tomorrow when it comes."

I took a few steps, then stopped and said, "Look up there. A single star."

"There's another one," Jelly said, pointing to the sky. It was like a painting. All around us, nothing but stillness, a quiet place. We walked along slowly, like a boy and his kid sister.

Upstairs he handed me a basin of warm water. "Wash your face," he said. Then he went out and returned with fresh water. "For your feet." He let me sleep in the bed, he took the sofa.

Up bright and early the next morning, I read for a long while, then walked out and found him sleeping in the master bedroom. His comforter had slid halfway off the bed. I carefully lifted it up and covered him. He opened his eyes. "Up so early?" I moved a stool up beside the bed and sat down. We talked a little, off and on. I told him I could see the lane out the window of his room, and that it reminded me of where I went for my first band interview.

I was fourteen at the time, and had just started liking rock 'n' roll. The band were no more than seventeen or eighteen.

It was winter. The two guitarists met me at the subway

birds soaring up from a thousand peaks

29

station and introduced me to the world of underground rock in their dark, dank, tiny room. It was also the first time I'd heard live music. I fell madly in love with the down-and-out, carefree, and slightly romantic atmosphere. I also started liking the lead guitarist, and after each session, I had to tear myself away.

Maybe it was my awkwardness or because they were young and shallow, but an argument erupted early on when I insisted that the guitarist walk me to the subway station one night. "You do this every time. You should try to be more independent," he muttered.

"Forget it, I'll go by myself," I said, even though I dreaded it. But then he was determined to take me. On the way over he kept up a steady stream of juvenile comments, comparing me with other journalists. When he finally ran out of things to say, I took off running. I never went back to see them again.

"Then what?" Jelly asked.

Then nothing. Unless you turned the clock back to when I was fourteen. When I was fourteen . . . I could picture what I looked like then: bobbed hair, a blue school uniform, an hour's subway ride every day to conduct interviews.

Jelly's mother made us breakfast. She was a good and kind woman who kept trying to get me to eat more. I loved the homey atmosphere and thought back to what Jelly had told me about his hometown in Sichuan. After stuffing ourselves, we went into his room, where he gave me a copy of *Red Star I*, which included Xu Wei's "Two Days". We listened to songs by Xu Wei and Hu Mage. "*God, what is it with us? God, what must they think of us?*" We cracked up over the corny lyrics.

Then it was Xu Wei: "*I let down my hair. Despair flowed over me like water.*" I was afraid to go home. What must my mother think of me?

At ten o'clock I said good-bye. I needed to go over to a guitar school. "Can't that wait till this afternoon? After lunch?" Jelly asked. I could tell he meant it, and I considered staying, but I had to leave. He walked me to where I'd parked my bike and gave me directions.

When I got to the Honghe Music School, Huang Ya was on the top floor practising the guitar. He told me to sit down and try my hand. I did, awkwardly.

"Do you practise?"

"Yes."

But I wasn't half as good at it as he was. He gave me some pointers, and I made up my mind to practise when I got home, so I wouldn't embarrass myself. I asked him where he was from. "Fujian," he said, and his heavy accent showed it. We talked a long time. He said that when he practised at home, they all complained of the noise.

"Can't you just ignore them?"

"Doesn't work," he said with a wry smile. "If I ignore my dad and my brothers I'm dead meat." He told me his father had come to Beijing to do business, and that he planned to form a rock band with his kid brother. Now all he had to do was convince the brother.

By that afternoon we were starving, so we went out to get some bread. I offered to buy a couple of hamburgers. "Fuck," he said. "That'll make me look cheap. I'll buy." Not bad.

"Do I seem shy to you?" he asked me. "Bashful?"

"Yes," I said.

"You know, back home I was never like this. People even said I was manic, abnormal. But I changed as soon as I got here, so much I don't even know myself anymore. Shy. Back in Fujian I had all kinds of friends, here I've only got a couple. . . ."

He said that when he first got here, he couldn't handle the Beijing dialect at all, and had to choose his words carefully. I asked him to say something in Fujianese, and what he came up with were some sounds I couldn't possibly write. He told me that was what the word "play" sounded like back home. When he saw how hard I was laughing, he said, "Sometimes you seem young for your age. Are you really as old as you say? I think you're just a kid!" I stared at him, wondering if that was a compliment or an insult. Maybe I did act like a kid around him.

"I'm surprised there is at least one cute, fun girl in this world," he said.

I blushed from excitement.

7 | THE WINTER OF YOUTH

My first semester in high school broke for vacation.

Naturally, all the students had to muster on the athletic field for a lecture by our big, fat political instructor, "Great Old Wang".

"Dance halls, discos and such are off-limits to students. There are places out there called something like 'Music for Learners' or 'Music for Yearners', that I tell you are no good. And don't go skating on the river, since I've heard reports that there was another drowning there recently! If you want to ice skate, ask your parents to let you take a couple of turns at the Capital Sports Arena. This school has had its share of problems. Three senior middle school students, Lei something, something Na, and . . . I won't divulge their names, to save them embarrassment, did nothing but play over the winter vacation, out dancing every night for over a week, and when they came back to school, their grades took a nosedive. Two of them barely managed to qualify for the high school entrance exam. The boy came back with a whole row of earrings and blond hair—a boy, mind you! Well, I sent him right home, because he'd turned into a regular hooligan!"

* * *

I was wearing filthy sneakers and blue jeans that fit snugly around my thighs, waiting for Ziyu under the overpass. I thought I was late, but he still hadn't showed up. In the white rays of the winter sun, I stood by the deserted road with my beat-up bike, not knowing what to do and feeling stupid about it.

Finally Ziyu rode up from the opposite direction, searching for me. I smiled playfully.

"Nice day," he said as he rode up carefully, looking straight ahead. My eyes were fixed on his mouth as his lips moved.

"What?"

"I said it's a nice day."

"Um."

Neither of us knew what to say, so we just rode along on our bikes.

"Let's check out the Jackie Bar first," I said after a prolonged silence. "Yang Zhiguo's band is playing."

"Okay. If it looks good, let's just chill there."

I figured he didn't want to pay the door charge at The Busy Bee. He was cheap, and I was getting tired of it.

The Jackie Bar was across the street from the Yanjing Hotel, so we kept our eyes peeled for the hotel. But we couldn't find it. He kept insisting it was just up ahead, until I stopped and asked someone, who told us we'd already passed it.

"I guess we ought to head back, don't you think?"

"No," I begged. "Let's go straight to The Busy Bee."

By the time we reached the club, my patience had run out, and I was looking forward to getting high on the music. That's all I wanted to do, listen to music, dance, and shout. No one was at the downstairs entrance. Maybe there wasn't a door charge, after all. That helped. But upstairs, at the bar entrance, a man with a broad grin was sitting at a table under a big white sign with red lettering that read: Door charge, fifty RMB. I got dizzy just looking at it. "Wow, that's high." I turned to look at Ziyu.

"Let me get it," he said reluctantly. "You don't have that kind of money."

That's what he always said when we had to pay for something. Maybe he expected me to be grateful for the way he puffed himself up by slapping his own cheeks. I took out some money—he didn't say a word as he handed over a hundred-RMB bill and took back the fifty I'd already given the doorman. We walked into the bar.

Like all bars, it was common for shows there to begin as much as an hour late. Ziyu bought two soft drinks. Thankfully not Pepsi, which damn near makes me puke.

Since the front rows were full, we sat at the back, near

the door. We needed to find a way to kill an hour, and when we looked at each other, it was obvious that wasn't going to be easy. We had nothing to talk about. We knew each other too well.

"How about Tianzi and the others, they here yet?" asked a familiar voice from behind. When I turned around, I saw Liu Feng, a friend from Cold Blooded Animals, one of the rock bands I'd interviewed.

"Liu Feng!" I shouted. He walked over and smiled. "It's . . . sorry, I've forgotten your name."

"That's okay!" I smiled back. "I'm Jiafu. Your hair's shorter."

"Oh, you're that journalist," he said, starting to warm up. "Now I remember. What are you up to these days?"

"Same as always," I said. We talked for a few minutes, and then I spotted Xie Tianxiao, Li Ming, and the others from the band. Their hair had gotten longer.

I started watching people who came and went, trying to guess their sex. Mostly rock musicians, they were wearing jeans, black or blue, and dark shirts. I saw one guy in a white shirt, and even though he sort of looked like a musician, his shirt gave him away as a college student. They all had a thing for white shirts. A campus poetry club, meetings out on the grass, shirts whiter than snow. . . .

The first band was Underbabies. I'd bought their album *Sartori* that very morning. Too bad they had to open the show, because it takes a while for audiences to get into the mood. Fact is, the audience never did warm up to them that night.

Ziyu and I elbowed our way up front, where we stood amid the swirling smoke.

When the third band came out, I was surprised to see that the college student in the white shirt was the lead singer. They sang passionately about love and ideals, about broken hearts their lovers could never appreciate; after each song they received thunderous "thanks and good-bye" applause from the audience, who then stared up at them sort of stupefied, waiting for them to realize that something was wrong and have enough self-awareness to get off the stage. But for some reason, maybe because getting any sort of gig was tough, they clutched their instruments and refused to leave. Meanwhile, the lead singer kept tossing his not-all-that-long hair, and I looked down, unable to bear watching him any longer.

The advertised band The Fly never made an appearance. After half listening to sets by several more shitty bands, my head felt like it was stuffed with cotton. The soft drink was making me sick, and all the smoke gave me a headache.

Cold Blooded Animals finally came onstage. The band, which Li Qi had said was an embarrassment to Shandong Province, sure made up for it that night. Xie Tianxiao's T-shirt, with a Union Jack on the back, showed off his bony arms. His guitar strap also sported a British flag. They played some songs I'd heard when I was interviewing them, and each one was followed by a long pause before the audience gathered their wits enough to start clapping. "Fucking awesome!" some guy behind me shouted out in a falsetto voice. I could tell it was Liu Feng.

During the break, I found a seat up front, which was a lot more comfortable until people stood up, and I couldn't see a thing. So I sat on the back of my chair with my feet on the seat. Ziyu sat on a table, feet touching the floor. Suddenly I overheard a guy nearby mention the name Jiang Xi, and remark that he was a terrific poet.

"Are you talking about the Jiang Xi who used to be with The Music Life?" I asked him. He looked at me, light glinting off his glasses. "That's the one! You know him? He's a great poet! A helluva lot better than people like Yi Sha."

"I like Yi Sha," I shot back.

"You know him?"

"He's an editor at the Xi'an magazine *Writers and Readers*, isn't he?"

"He's in Beijing now."

"Say what?"

"He's got a poetry reading at Number 52 tomorrow."

A few minutes later, Specs brought a beer over and sat down beside me. "Where do you go to school?"

"Beida."

He gave me a suspicious look. "What year?"

"Freshman."

"What's your major?"

"Journalism."

He looked at me doubtfully. "Which dorm you live in?"

"I commute," I explained, then burst out laughing. "I'm a high school freshman."

"I thought you said you're in college?"

"Just fooling around," I said. "What about you?"

"I'm at Beida. . . ."

"Shit!" I cursed under my breath. He didn't look it. Didn't have that whatever-it-was. When he saw I was staring at him, he said, "Okay, the PLA Art Academy." He showed off his uniform pants, and I had to admit, it was a good-looking uniform. Then he showed me his student ID. I still wasn't sure I believed him, so I studied the photo. It was him, all right.

"You here alone?" he asked.

I hesitated for a moment, then pointed to Ziyu. "I'm with a friend."

"Oh!" He pulled his hand back and started to say something, but didn't. He looked hilarious.

I still had a headache, so I went outside for some air. It was freezing, and I guessed it must have been past midnight. I only stayed out a few minutes before going back upstairs. When I got to the table, Specs walked back over.

"My name's Shi Jun," he said. "What's yours?"

I thought for a minute. "Here, I'll write it for you."

He handed me his address book, which was filled with names. I found a space and wrote mine. I stopped, then added my phone number.

"Lin Jiafu," he read.

"It's hard to talk in here," he said. "What do you say we go outside for a walk?"

As we were walking downstairs, I said, "I couldn't stand that earlier band! All that love this, love that was driving me crazy!"

"What does a fifteen-year-old know about love?" he asked as he walked beside me.

I ignored the comment.

"6684 XXXX," he read as he took his address book out. "6684, that's a military exchange, isn't it?"

"Yeah."

"So your father must be in one of those rear-service units."

"I'm not sure, but I think he's a member of the Central Guard Regiment."

"Hey, somebody's written something on that car over there." He was right, there was a bunch of stuff written all over it.

"Want to write something?" he asked.

"No."

"Then I will." He reached out and etched the words "Jiafu baby" on the filthy windshield.

We started walking again.

"How much do you weigh?" he asked.

What could I say? "I haven't weighed myself lately. Maybe I'll do that tomorrow."

"No need." He grabbed me from behind and picked me up. I kicked and squirmed.

"You're pretty heavy!" he said. Heavy would have been just fine, no need to add "pretty".

He put me down, bent over, and, before I knew what was happening, he was kissing me. I was more than surprised, I was pissed. I pulled away and pointed a finger at him. "Why you . . ."

"Why you . . ." Shi Jun mimicked me.

I started walking again, sulking. He didn't say anything, and before long, neither one of us knew what to say. "That is so . . . why'd you do that? . . ." I sighed softly. My reactions were too damn slow.

The next time he kissed me, I said softly, "I don't even know you."

"You do now," he said as he led me over to a corner.

We held each other, but that left me cold. That thing of his was right up against my thigh, hard as a rock.

After a while, Shi said sombrely, "Once at a literary gathering, Wang Shuo said, 'I don't buy that act of yours, so I'll take you to bed.'"

My dear, dear friend, how come it took you so long to get to the point?

* * *

"It's getting cold," he said. "We'd better go get a coat."

It was freezing, so we headed back to the bar.

"Are you really at the PLA Art Academy?" I asked him.

"Yeah. Why?"

No reason. I envied him.

When we got upstairs, Ziyu was still sitting on the table. He looked lonely as he watched me walk over.

"By the time 43 Baojia Street took the stage, half the audience had already left," he said.

"Really?" I laughed. "I like their skinny keyboard player."

"How come?"

"He's cute in a wimpy sort of way."

We didn't talk on the way back home. I wanted to tell Ziyu what had happened, but I didn't know where to start.

I had all kinds of crazy thoughts that night, but I knew that the next time I went back to the club, it would be like nothing had happened.

Li, these words are my gift to you!

There's one kind of feeling that depresses me
And my life is mired in that feeling
I think of this when in transit, and I'm resentful
I don't know how to express it
I've never been much of a poet

It's that I want to kill you
And let you know
That I want to kill you
I've already seen through everything you do

One day I will kill you
Just you wait

One day after school was back in session I received a totally unexpected phone call from Li Qi. A million things I wanted to say flooded my mind, the strongest of which was "You motherfucker!" But I held back. He said he was back in town, like he was doing me a big favour, and like it was only yesterday we'd been together. God, how I hated that.

Eventually he got around to asking if I was busy Saturday, that he'd like me to go to his place. Disgusting. But I thought that the day had finally arrived when I could gain some closure.

After hanging up, I noted that I was grinning from ear to ear. That really blew me away. God! As if I'd been hoping he'd return to Beijing, as if I'd been waiting for that phone call all along. . . .

* * *

Early morning. Like all Saturday mornings back then. The subway, to Jishuitan. For three months I'd made this trip every Saturday morning to see him, nervously, fearfully hoping to keep the relationship going. Now, another Saturday, another visit.

The subway crept along, but I was calm as could be. I'd waited this long already, so what difference could another hour or so make?

I stepped silently onto the escalator, which took me to ground level, and then I walked down the left-hand side of the street, watching other people hurry past. I was feeling smug and somewhat lost at the same time. But overshadowing both feelings was the secure knowledge that I was in control this time. The Xu Beihong Museum, his school. Up ahead, the lane across from the music and video shop.

You lean up against the wall breathing heavily. You walk into the compound; there's no one around, but you're still panicky. Like you're afraid someone will see you. You knock lightly at the door. It opens, and you slip inside. Your eyes meet, and you actually feel a little embarrassed. The abject feelings that had long since vanished come drifting back before you know it. You damn near say "Good morning," but he doesn't even acknowledge your presence. After a fleeting glance, he closes his eyes and goes back to sleep. Anger over being brushed off like that leads to crippling remorse. You're suspended in midair, mortified, but just like the last time, all the curses die on your lips.

* * *

As soon as the door opens, you take out a knife, and go at him. Your victim has no time to react. Ah! Ah! Ah! Each thrust is accompanied by radiant peals of laughter as his blood throws a red veil over your face. Finally you tumble into the pool of blood. You see the roll of toilet paper wiping clean the blood of your young girl's chastity. You use the toilet paper to wipe the blood off the knife, jerk open the door, and leave. You've done something for yourself at last.

* * *

The truth is, when I saw Li, not only did I not curse him, I actually stood there stammering and muttering, as if instead of resolving the matter, the matter had resolved me. "Have a seat," he said, pointing to the blanket covering him in bed. "No thanks," I replied.

I spotted a backpack hanging on the wall, obviously the one he'd carried to Guangzhou. I couldn't help thinking about him and his girlfriend doing it. Of course they had sex. The thought made my chest seize up, something spongy slowly working its way under my ribs.

"How come you took off for Guangzhou without telling me?" I asked him.

"I wasn't going to go at first, even on the day I bought my train ticket. I tried to cash it in, but when I called the station, they said there was a five percent penalty, fifty RMB altogether. That didn't seem worth it, so I went."

"I'm sure you had a wonderful time," I said sarcastically.

"Yeah, I'd say so."

When I pictured Cai Yun beaming happily when she saw him, envisioned their intimate movements as they made love, the sad look in her eyes when he left, I nearly choked with anger. That and his self-righteous manner as he lay in bed just about took my breath away. He was having a great time.

"It's not easy for Cai Yun, living all alone in Guangzhou. No money to go home for New Year's, and since she wasn't going, I certainly wasn't either. I didn't want her to be depressed."

How noble.

I still found it hard to understand Li's accent, and now whatever tenderness I'd felt at first was gone. I kept hoping he'd say something with feeling, even call me an idiot if he felt like it. But, no, not a true word from this deep individual, this "artiste". He wouldn't even get out from under the covers, he just looked up at me with those benevolent eyes. There was nothing I could do. Later on, when I thought back, I understood that his attitude was really just total indifference: Go ahead, get excited if you want, it doesn't bother me. If you scream obscenities at me, I'll do what I can to soothe you, because I'm just entirely apathetic.

I sat there in his cramped room that day wondering why I'd come in the first place. Given the overall atmosphere, pitching some sort of fit would have been imbecilic, but I couldn't help it if an absurd half smile crept onto my face, like some belligerent punk.

Li said I'd be well advised to change my personality.

Well, fuck you! You think you're hot shit, don't you? What I do is my business. Who needs you to grace me with your words of wisdom from on high? I'll be as wild as I want to be.

Afterwards, I walked down the street just looking for a fight. How had I ever got mixed up with someone like that? I was looking for a stand-up guy and wound up with a complete asshole, a master at evasion.

From the moment this pathetic hoodlum showed up on the streets of Beijing, all sorts of good-hearted people helped him out. In the heart of our motherland's artistic circles, his family paid his rent, his pals pitched in with food. The country was populated by girls who had been tricked into falling for his phony idealism and hung around waiting for him. . . . With his bourgeois mentality and proletarian identity, this heartless self-styled artiste never did anything worthwhile except eat and wait for the sun to set. How did he have the guts to go on living?

From the day I stepped uneasily into his room until the time I fled from embarrassment, I never did say the two things I'd come prepared to say: "Have you been playing with me all along?" and "You motherfucker!" Saying them might have been shallow; but not saying them could also be interpreted that way, so maybe I should have gone ahead and said them. What did that make me? A goddamn idiot? All my anger had been defused by Li's indifference, his ability to do only what was necessary to get the job done, and no more. I was the loser.

When I got back home, I reread all my letters to Li, which he'd returned to me. The very first one I'd written; the simple English one I'd pounded out the previous semester in typing class; the one I'd written a week before getting his last letter, in which I'd poured out all my longings and plans . . . among them was a letter Cai Yun had written to him, which he'd probably overlooked. It was neatly written in pencil, and dealt with the first time they'd said good-bye, and there was this line: "As the train pulled out of the station, I saw that you too were shedding quiet tears. . . ." It was emotionally charged, one of those passionate love letters boyfriends and girlfriends are always sending to one another. I read it carefully, over and over, then burned it along with all of mine.

2

born at the wrong time

West X High, the school I tried so hard to leave, and feared I never could. In my two and a half years of wallowing there I felt like I was using up every ounce of energy and passion I had. Even up to the day I knew that I never again had to go back, it still invaded my dreams, turned them into nightmares.

I pushed my bike into the school yard on the first day of class and was immediately confronted by two class monitors, one named Li, the other called Big-Belly Wang. They were smiling, but I could see it was all an act, like maybe they were inspecting troops. "Hey, there, student. Take your bicycle outside and come back in again!" Big-Belly Wang said. What'd I do? Totally puzzled, I pushed my bike out the gate and watched to see how the other students entered: They all bowed to the teachers and greeted them with "How do you do, teachers!" The monitors "kindly" returned the bows. The two of them, a man and a woman, had mastered the imperial wave of national leaders, quite a pair. I got the picture. Swallowing my anger and embarrassment, I pushed my bike back inside. "How do you do, teachers!" They smiled. "Good morning." I was so goddamned disgusted I felt like puking.

The tuition there was high—thirteen hundred RMB—and with all the added fees, it came to nearly two thousand, which was a lot more than I'd paid for three years of middle school. The tuition was so damned high that I made up my mind to work hard at my studies. Brave words welled up inside me, and sort of hung around for a moment, before slipping away.

The morning and midday inspections during the first month were devoted to studying school regulations, a long-standing tradition. Every first-year student was given a twenty-four-page pamphlet, no exception, which we studied in the mornings and were tested on at midday. Its full title was "Beijing West X Vocational High School Rules of Student Governance", and it was divided into eleven chapters—Instruction, Character Standards, Proper Behaviour, Classroom Study, Classroom Activity, Hygiene, Personal Property, Attendance, Student Status, Progress Awards, Discipline—plus the following appendices: (1) Evaluation and Selection of Outstanding Class, 'Three Good' Students, and Outstanding Cadres;(2) Evaluation of Students' Daily Behaviour; and (3) Evaluation of Classes' Daily Behaviour.

The professional standards for Foreign Affairs PR Copy Secretary majors were:

Observe discipline and guard secrets; maintain good, positive work habits; greet others with a smile; be dignified and appropriate in appearance; and be refined and poised in behaviour.

Possess complete mastery of vocational abilities: coherent, intelligible verbal skills; cordial, genial PR skills; ability to write practical, smooth official documents; relatively good English conversational skills; proficiency with machinery (including Chinese and English typing); relatively accomplished penmanship and calligraphy; and basic filing and stenographic skills.

* * *

Upon graduation, the following certificates would be awarded: General Secretarial, Typing, and Word Processing.

There was even a poem about proper behaviour patched together by someone in the school's leadership, maybe by Principal Pan, who was an outstanding specimen:

Manner and looks crucial, you must know how.
Four rhyming-word codes, let's hear them now.
Sit proper legs crossed, knees ready to kowtow.
Stand squarely stretch tall, no jelly-bellied sow.
Stride steadily and strong, straight like a plough.
Face earthy and clean, do not paint your brow.
Nice natural hair style, not some furry chow.
Warmly cordial to others, say hello and bow.
Speak genially and softly, smile and say ciao.

Good to associate with, never cause any row.
Think pure noble thoughts, lofty goals a vow.
Be cultivated and polite, meek like a meooow.
Elegant and eternally poised, don't have a cow.

There were, in addition, the following absolutely incomprehensible regulations: No visiting other classrooms (Classroom Activity Regulation 7); Students from other schools may not wait for local students outside the school yard, and if they are caught, the students they are waiting for will be punished (Classroom Activity Regulation 11); Students must eat lunch at school, and may not go outside to buy food (same as above); Students who wish to go home for lunch must bring a note from their parents, who must make themselves aware of the students' lunch-hour activities (same as above); students who go home for lunch must arrange for a special pass to be shown at the gate when leaving and reentering (same as above). Then there were slogans like "Neatness Is Discipline". No loitering in the hallways, no mail sent to school, no outside books; even missing class with cause or for sickness led to grade deductions. There were monthly schoolwide exams and no makeup. . . .

But the workload was light, and there was little homework. The first year in high school is supposed to be pretty relaxed, a time to enjoy life. And the pressure of exams is even lower in vocational high schools. Everything's always easy at first. There were, however, two courses that drove us nuts: Etiquette and Posture and Fitness. Principal Pan personally taught the etiquette course. If you stared at her ghostly pale face long enough, she looked like an animal—a fox. For the P & F class, we had to wear tight gym suits, and there was never enough time between classes to change in and out of them. We hated it.

10 | MY FIRST-YEAR CLASS (SECTION 6)

My life during that first year was a series of new beginnings. The time just flew by. There was more going on than I could deal with. The air in the western suburbs was clean, the sky blue every day, like silver. My class monitor was wonderful to me because I gained a reputation as a good student—I wrote poems, I painted, I studied, I organized activities, and I was determined to work hard and not waste my three years here, since I was intent on getting into the school of my dreams—Beida. After the last two classes were over in the afternoons, I, along with my friend Xie Sini and some other girls, rode home on our bikes. It was autumn, Beijing's golden season. When the weather was fine and the air clean, outlines of the distant mountains sprang into view, and we sang Shen Qing's song: "A blue, blue sky above the red, red sun . . ." A distant, youthful joy enveloped us. It was like the brief honeymoon that launches a long marriage. Compared to the days that followed, this was the golden period of my entire school life.

Whenever I had the time, I went over to Beida or the Haidian Book City. Beida. Beautiful. That's it in a nutshell. Xie Sini said it was like a park. "It's much prettier than a park," I said proudly. At the time, Beida was even prettier than it had been when I visited it in the autumn of my third year in middle school. There was an exhibition of photographs by the Mountain Eagle Society, plus all kinds of charity sales and recruiting booths for clubs. Once again, I felt as clearly as was humanly possible that if I belonged to Beida (I no longer entertained the thought that Beida would belong to me), I would be unbelievably happy.

There were only twenty-seven students in my class, twenty-two of them girls. Five boys in a class was the lowest ratio in the school. But these five were special—they were active, funny, and they could talk a blue streak. And they all had a touch of melancholy.

We paid 120 RMB for lunch, and got a card. Not the meal cards you got in college, the kind you swiped, but thin pieces of paper that a member of the student association checked each time you used it. And if you forgot yours, well, tut-tut, no food for you, and don't blame the school leadership. The one thing you didn't want to do was act put out and remind them that everyone had to pay the fee and eat campus food, because you'd be wasting your breath. Whether you ate or not was your business, and since you'd chosen this school, you were expected to follow its rules. Some of the students couldn't understand what the cards were for in the first place. Nothing, they were told, but you'd better show yours at lunchtime; and if you've lost it, you'll have to scrounge up five RMB for a replacement. Since our pitifully small cafeteria could only accommodate a few classes at a time on a rotating basis, we had to queue up on the basketball court to wait our turn to buy lunch. Objectively speaking, the food wasn't bad: two dishes, one meat and one vegetarian, and in every three-day period, we ate steamed buns twice and rice once. Sometimes we found sand and tiny pebbles in the rice, but that was no big deal, and even the occasional sliver of glass or small nail didn't raise an eyebrow.

About a month after classes began, a new student was assigned to Section 6. At our midday inspection, Teacher Wang walked in with a girl. "This is Du Yuan. Section 6 now has a new member." The new girl introduced herself in a low, throaty voice. She said she liked dancing and art, and that was all. Public speaking seemed to make her nervous.

The new girl acquired star status almost immediately. All the students in our school had to wear their hair short, and girls were expected to part theirs down the middle. Hers was short, but she parted it on the side. We all wore the same uniform, but she added a scarf around her neck, brown with white polka dots and probably no more expensive than those you can buy on street corners. But that silk scarf drew our attention like a magnet. It started a fad. And even though our silk or satin scarves might have cost more than hers, on her it just seemed more fitting, more natural. The truth is, I never got very close to her. She was an enigma. She didn't participate in any of our military drills. Someone said she was from Xi'an, and that she lived in Beijing with her grandfather.

She reminded me of some of the characters I'd invented, and on several occasions I imagined her as a girl who existed only in my fantasies.

* * *

The school required each grade to organize a class activity with a special theme. The theme for first-year students was

"I love my major." "I'm giving this assignment to you, Jiafu," Teacher Wang said to me. So I asked Ziyu to make a tape with Luo Dayou, The Beatles, Queen, Yu Dong, and Gao Xiaosong for background music, then I copied passages from novels about school, concentrating on stirring passages that glorified youth. Other students signed up to participate, thanks to the five to ten points awarded for each performance, and the show was a roaring success. Du Yuan performed a dance, and it wasn't until then that we realized how thin a waist she had. She wore this lovely expression while she danced, and had tied a ribbon of cloth around her waist, so thin it looked like it might fall off at any minute. It never did. The grade monitor and two outside judges, all male, stared at her, grinning from ear to ear. But our class monitor looked at me, not her, since I was her favourite, her most talented student.

Sometimes the school organized other activities in the current popular phrase of "going with a concept". Each had a clearly defined theme, such as "military training report-back performances" or "knowledge bowls", but the actual nature and substance were ignored. The problem was, I began to realize that the students at my school were extremely ill-informed. For example, during the knowledge bowl, if you asked who wrote the classic lines "Up to Heaven, down to Earth, on to the Yellow Springs/Two vast realms, in neither did he find her", the third-year students would sit there mute until someone would actually ask if such a poem had ever been written. If one of them managed to answer the question, "What's the smallest bird on earth?" the audience would buzz. Shit, to think that someone so smart actually attends our school! It was astonishing! I was bored having to function in this environment. There was no campus culture to speak of.

So after a while going to school every day became exhausting, and all I wanted to do when I got home was sleep—a luxury I didn't have. In the summer following my graduation from middle school, I had interviewed four underground rock bands for a music magazine, and now I had to hurry and put the finished interviews into publishable form. And I had to practise the guitar to keep from lagging behind. Plus, every first-year student was required to write an "autobiography", a "self-confession" of a thousand words or more. "I want to chill out by myself, I don't want to go on living, I feel like lying down and never getting up again. . . ." They'd shoot me if I wrote that.

Hypocrisy was my only choice: "Life is bright and sunny, 21st century, a generation striding into a new century, the future . . ." You have to be fucking kidding.

1 1 | OLD ROSES IN A ROSE GARDEN

Another spring came and is on its way out.

Another spring wasted.

They'd just turned off the heating, and I was still wearing winter clothes. I hate being cold. Getting through the period when the temperature is rising but there's still a chill in the air just about does me in, even though winter is my favourite season. Little Yang from the band Faithless Babes said he'd had a lot of work recently, that his days were just packed, and

I was glad to hear it. Energetic people with plenty to do should be out doing it. I had nothing special to do except indulge my fantasies and read books. For several weeks in a row I raced home on my bike on Thursday afternoons to catch the TV programme *Very English*, hoping there'd be some rock music that I'd like. That was the only thing that broke up my boredom.

I've never been someone who has goals. Never. And even with a rosy veil over my eyes, I couldn't see the future.

* * *

There was a slight drizzle one Wednesday morning, and after waking up, I sat in bed in my rumpled PJs, not wanting to move.... What to do? ... True freedom has never existed in this world ... should I transfer? ... drop out of school? ... The flowers in spring, the winds of autumn, and the setting sun of winter ... these were the silly thoughts of a melancholy young girl.... Finally I managed to drag myself out the door, knowing that I was going to be late. It only took a second to decide what I was going to do. I pedalled past The Ark Bookstore, then circled back. It hadn't opened yet, so I rode over to the post office on Suzhou Avenue. Surrounded by the ringing of bicycle bells, I seemed to be the only carefree person around. At the post office I picked up the March issue of *The College Student* and flipped through it. My eye was caught by a poem written by the guy I'd run into at The Busy Bee, the "young poet" from the PLA Arts Academy, Shi Jun. "What happened that night isn't something I ought to be talking about," he'd written. What a joke! He'd actually used words like "love" and "degenerate". No irony intended. I felt like calling him up and giving him this poetic line: "A shitty poem by a fucked-up person." The poet Yi Sha said it: In a rose garden an old rose like him will always be the enemy of rock 'n' roll.

I thought about calling up some friends that morning, but didn't. I wanted them to see me when I was cutting a sorry figure, all confused, and actually treat me to breakfast, then drag me off to relax with a book or take in some music, when in fact they'd probably be pissed off at being disturbed and pepper me with questions about why I wasn't in school, and end up trying to talk some sense into me.

For skipping school that day, I got my mother to write a note, and since my class monitor was partial to me, nothing happened. But in the days that followed, my disgust with the school grew stronger, and I regularly showed up late or cut classes, until the school laid down the law, requiring from me the "three musts" for an approved absence: a note from home, a note from a doctor, and a prescription, no exceptions.

12 | FEEBLE SOBS

I was getting fed up with talking and all other forms of self-expression. I did everything possible to avoid contact with vacuous people.

I went out walking with Jelly. First we went to Earth Temple Park, where he'd interviewed the rock vocalist and songwriter Pu Shu a few days earlier. There was a chill in the air, so he took off his denim jacket and gave it to me. We found the bench where he'd conducted the interview, and Jelly told me Pu Shu had written some lyrics on the ground that day, but neither of us could find them, no matter how carefully we looked.

I brought up the name of a certain music critic. "Didn't you hear? He killed himself not long ago," Jelly said.

"He did?" I asked excitedly. "How come?"

"Don't know."

I really admired the guy's courage, and if I'd known he was thinking about suicide, instead of trying to talk him out of it I'd have had a good long conversation with him. I don't know why, but I've got this crude idea that anybody who fucking scorns life, who sees life as a pile of shit, who feels that life is meaningless and offers nothing but constant suffering, is fearless, courageous . . . in a word, cultivated. See, that's what gets me going. I'm a pessimist down to the marrow of my bones. Jelly once wrote an essay that I stumbled across one rainy day on the top floor of the Honghe Music School; it was in an old issue of a music journal. Here's part of what he wrote:

Whenever I'm about to leave the house, I check for my room key, my address book, which has the phone numbers of everyone I know in the city, the floppy disks with all my writing, my pager, and my bus pass. If any of them are missing, I can't leave the house. But then, once when I took a train on a long trip, I realized that not one of those things was absolutely essential.

Sometimes I know of people who have passed on, and I grieve for the dead and for their loved ones. But the dead no longer exist and have taken their memories with them, while

the ones they've left behind will cease their mourning one day
and start getting used to life without them. As with a pebble
tossed into a lake, the ripples will spread farther and farther
until they disappear. At times like this, the realization comes
to me that there is no absolute necessity for life.

There is no absolute necessity for life.

I don't much like Jelly's recent essays. He has lost the ability to turn common sentiments into serious writing. But in his early work, the depth of his sincerity is painful and exhilarating. He captures the beauty of desolation and annihilation. Reality makes people lose hope, so I think the way most men and boys hold passionately and stubbornly to life is disconcerting. How can they love life so much? When I read Jelly's essay, I picked up the phone and called him, since he was the first man I'd ever known who actually detested life. I liked that. Maybe I'm just naturally oversensitive, but I yearned to find a kindred spirit.

* * *

We went out to eat, and once we were in the taxi, a soft rain began to fall; the neon lights behind the rain made it incredibly visible. We went to a fast-food restaurant, where we sat down in a booth by a window. After the food came, Jelly asked me how things were at home.

"For me it's sheer torture, for them devastation."

After a while I started talking about conducting interviews, and I got so emotional I started to cry. I was telling him about a time I went to interview the band, Inductive Agency, alone and without knowing what I was doing, and all of a sudden I lost it. Jelly handed me a tissue, and I said, "Don't look at me!"

He smiled and, sounding both tired and caring at the same time, said, "I envy you. I haven't cried in a very long time. You're very mature."

"No, I'm not," I replied.

"Then life's going to be hard for you."

"I won't live long."

"How long do you plan to live?"

"Who knows? At least into the twenty-first century."

Jelly said I asked too much of life. But how was I to ask too little?

As we got onto the subway, he said abruptly, "Are you in a vocational high school?"

Sparks flew from my eyes.

"Yes, I'm in a vocational high school, but I want to go to Beida. You think that's bordering on the impossible? I want to become a top journalist, and I'm going to Beida."

Jelly looked down and took out an envelope. "Here," he said, "this is for you. You'll pass the entrance exam for sure. Beida's the school for people like you. If you can't get in, nobody can. Sensitive little thing." I opened the envelope. Inside were a photo of Xu Wei in a performance on April 8 and three blown-up promotional photos of him.

* * *

My future scared me; I didn't want to suffer. But suffering and joy have always been pretty much the same thing to me. Whenever I'm enjoying life, the cost is its opposite. So the only way to avoid suffering was to rid my life of joy. It all boiled down to one word: Death. No feelings. The land of ultimate bliss. Nirvana. I wanted absolute nothingness.

I cried because I was going out on a date and had no new pants and no decent shoes.

I cried because an electric guitar cost fifteen hundred RMB, more than I could afford.

My room was an empty chamber. No friends. I hated lonely Sunday afternoons. I lay there and sobbed weakly, felt consigned to permanent weakness. I despised everything I saw. After I'd cried myself out, I felt cold. I hated myself.

I know there are lots of people who can't stand dark writing with a decadent tone, you know, like writing about yourself as if writing about others. If you're one of them, stop here. I'm not going to force you.

13 | BORN TO BE A PILOT

I hated school more and more each day. I didn't want to study that shit anymore, didn't want to waste any more time there. I'd had about all I could take of the place. Just the thought of two more years there drove me up the wall. Thoughts of my final exam, plus exams on clerical work, shorthand, P & F, computer, made my head swell. I looked up at the mother hen standing at the front of the room and wondered what he'd come here for . . . I wanted to go to college, I wanted to be alone. If I stuck it out at this school, would there be anything left of me? Assigned a job, going to work, entrance exams . . . I'd die of exhaustion. The only subjects that interested me were language and politics, but my history teacher also taught second-year photography, so there'd be no history class my second semester. My life was like an unguided missile, and I figured that sooner or later I'd crash and be smashed to pieces. Teacher Wang wrote in my journal, "Why must you always disparage the qualities and abilities of people your own age?" There was a haughty tone to her question. Not true, I didn't do that; it's just that I felt that high school students lacked unity.

I hated my school but liked the class I was assigned to. To be more precise, I liked the sluggish, decadent, somewhat sugary atmosphere, and I liked some of my classmates and teachers. I was grateful to the class monitor, Teacher Wang, for making so many things easy for me. In that harsh environment, I was relatively free, thanks to her. Despite the fact that I was no longer easily moved, I was touched. I think she must have understood my appreciation.

Towards the end of my fifteenth year, during Beijing's rotten spring, I bumped into painful reality time and again as I chased my dreams. I knew that my thoughts were all over the place, but they never lacked clarity. I knew exactly what I wanted and what I was doing.

What I needed now was to take care of myself.

I needed room to do what I wanted without interfering with anybody, free to do as I pleased.

I got to know a band from Kaifeng who called themselves SpermOva. The members of SpermOva sent me some black-and-white publicity photos, all featuring Jia Jia. The pictures were shot at a school, in condemned buildings, on Kaifeng streets, and in front of their homes. The band consisted of Bai Jianqiu (bass), Wei Ruixian (guitar), Jia Jia (lead singer, guitar), and Li Zhanwu (drums).

"Come to Kaifeng," they said. "We're here waiting for you."

I really, really loved that band and dreamed of walking down the streets of Kaifeng with them. I wanted to go there, I wanted to break out of this school, I wanted to go and see them in Kaifeng, where we'd have a million things to talk about. My mind was made up. I was going there.

My mother found a guidance counsellor for me, and wanted me to see him on Saturday or Sunday, but I was defiant. There's nothing wrong with my head, why should I see a shrink? But then I thought, why not? If the psychiatrist could figure me out, who knows, he might talk my mother into giving me more freedom.

We wore short sleeves and hats on the blistering summer day we went to see the guidance counsellor. After getting off the 375 bus, we had a long walk to the Qinghua University High School, where the counselling office was located. Some of the dorm students hadn't yet left, and we were treated to the sight of hot-blooded kids happily running around. We went to the third floor mental health office in a small building, where we were greeted by a teacher with long hair. After we timidly took the seats we were offered, she poured us some hot water. We chatted a while, then she asked us to wait while she attended a meeting.

Mother and I sipped our water on the sofa, while I flipped through a stack of *Beijing Youth*. The green canopies of poplars bent in the wind and brushed against the window, and I could hear the shouts and laughter of students downstairs. I had a funny feeling: When had I lost my student's sense of innocence?

About an hour later, the teacher returned and said with an embarrassed smile, "Sorry to keep you waiting."

"No problem."

"Let's go into the other room," she said. The new room was much cozier than the first, and better furnished. "Would you like some coffee?" she asked.

"No, thanks, water is fine," I said. I liked her right off; she had a considerate, warm quality that earned my immediate trust. I told her about wanting to go to Kaifeng to see the band SpermOva, and she thought that was a good idea. Could I wait till summer vacation? I said I didn't want to wait even another day. She was on my side, but she tried to get me to compromise. I knew she was right, that she was just being practical, that waiting for summer vacation was the sensible thing to do. My mother even chipped in with the suggestion that the band could come to Beijing during summer vacation, at my parents' expense. But it didn't work.

The teacher reminded me how upset I would be if I went to Kaifeng and SpermOva turned out to be a disappointment, nothing like I'd expected.

I said I'd be prepared for that.

She smiled at Mother and just shrugged her shoulders.

I left Qinghua University High reluctantly. It impressed me as a terrific school. Big, beautiful, a great campus, lots of energetic students, and kind teachers. Just what I thought a high school ought to be.

Birds flew noisily over the campus grounds. The sky was a deep blue.

14 | FAIFENG, THE NIGHT IS STILL YOUNG

Mother and I went to buy train tickets. I filled my backpack with CDs and newspapers for the trip, but it seemed as if we'd travelled to hell and back before the train finally reached Shangqiu Station, just before Kaifeng.

The setting sun sent down beautiful golden rays of sunshine from the edge of the sky, reminding me of the classic lines: "A solitary plume of smoke in the desert/The rounded sun setting over the Yangtze." I went back to an empty car and sat down by myself, letting the sunbeams wash over my body, my face, and the cocoon of joy all around me, body and soul.

After stepping down off the train, my heart seemed about to burst out of my chest. I wondered where they might be waiting for me. "SpermOva!" I shouted.

No one answered in the darkness. Mother and I walked out of the station, then spotted four people at the foot of the steps. I rushed over. "Are you Jiafu?" one of them asked. I nodded and reached out to shake hands. That took him by surprise, but he stuck out his hand. I later learned that he was the bass player, Jianqiu. After my ID was checked, Jia Jia came up and hugged me, appearing warm and a little wary at the same time, maybe because my mother was there with me.

First we went to the home of Li Zhanwu, the drummer. Not a bad place, if you ask me. In some respects, an improvement over comparable apartments in Beijing. Li's mother was a typical middle-class urbanite. She spoke Mandarin pretty well, but I think she went a little overboard in welcoming us, which made me sort of uneasy. We all sat down to dinner at about nine o'clock. Obviously, there was a lot I wanted to say, and I finally got permission to spend the night with SpermOva in Li Zhanwu's apartment. We all walked there together. Kaifeng's streets are narrow and dark, and as I walked along I suddenly felt that something wasn't quite right. This was the city I'd dreamed about and fought to visit for so long; why wasn't I just about passing out from excitement? So I shouted, "Wow, here I am in Kaifeng! This is Kaifeng!"

To get to Li Zhanwu's place we had to cross some railroad tracks. The scene was new and magnificent, with trains passing through town and airplanes flying so low you could see their red lights. It was an aging but well-equipped apartment: a bed (including blankets and pillows), a balcony, a water heater, a toilet, even an old radio. As soon as I got there, I dumped all my CDs and newspapers on the bed, but that didn't get the reaction I'd expected. Here's how I wanted it to be: All of us lying in bed, arms around each other as we listened to rock music in the dark and talked about all sorts of things. That was the sort of intimacy I'd yearned for. But it's not how things turned out. I was sleepy, but they were still in high spirits, so they turned on all the lights and played loud music, each doing one thing or another, leaving me as the outsider, alone. What I wanted was to lie with my arms around Jia Jia or, for that matter, any of my friends. I really needed that feeling. A warm feeling. I touched Jia Jia's hand. "I want to hold your hand," I said. My mood was exactly like that in the Beatles' song. He was unmoved. Humiliation washed over me.

To hell with being rational—all I wanted was to follow my emotions. I understood that letting my emotions run free wasn't a good idea, that it could only mess things up. That was obvious, even then. But emotions are hard to control. Too hard, in fact. My heart was so spongy it sapped my energy. I felt powerless.

By about two in the morning everyone was tired. Li Zhanwu and Bai Jianqiu took the sofa. Jia Jia, Wei Ruixian, Jin Zhiheng, and I slept on the bed. The lights were turned off. Before we went to sleep, the lead guitarist, Wei Ruixian, told a bunch of dirty jokes, and we all laughed. I held Jia Jia's hand, hoping to feel something warm and dependable. He let me put it wherever I wanted, displaying no emotion whatsoever. For me that was sheer misery! The only possible explanation was that he (or they) had no feelings for me at all. God, what an idiot I was! Why was I always so sure of myself? Why were my feelings never appreciated? Why am I always the one who gets hurt? Caught up in these thoughts, I drifted off into an uneasy sleep.

The moment my eyes opened in the morning, all I wanted was to get back to Beijing as soon as humanly possible. Just take off. But I knew that was out of the question. I felt like screaming, but I was in somebody else's goddamn apartment.

I couldn't keep from heaving a sigh. I felt like going up to Jia Jia and asking him, Do you even consider me a friend?

15 | A FLASH

The next day felt even longer. Soon after I got up in the morning, Mother and Aunty Li (Li Zhanwu's mother) came over, and that was pretty awkward. We ate oil fritters, which made me thirsty. Jia Jia slept like a dead man, like there was no waking him.

Later that morning I went out onto the balcony to take in the view. Thick, tall parasol trees grew there, the air smelled like tofu. Li Zhanwu later told me there was a pharmaceutical plant nearby.

Li, the drummer, and I got along great. He said his mother might send him to Kaifeng University in a few months to study computers. I gave him a ten-RMB Luo Dayou CD. I hit it off with Bai Jianqiu too. And yet I was still in a funk. The unity, purity, and infatuation you expect with a true comrade, they couldn't give me. I wanted nothing more than to talk openly about the tough issues of life, music, and ideals, or anything else, with people, but there was no one.

Before coming, every thought of the band had made me happy, had made me smile; now there was only fright and a sense of danger. How could it have turned out like this? It was real. My prior happiness was real, but so was my present distress.

The third day they took me to see their school, a vocational high school in a white building. The athletic field and the roof were covered with green moss, and both were a lot bigger than West X High. Students on the athletic field were in summer uniforms; the boys were playing soccer, the girls were just talking in groups. They were all so lively, so full of youth. The sun was bright as I walked up to their classroom and, gathering my courage, stepped inside. Some of the girls acted surprised when they saw me, probably wondering who this new girl was, since they'd never seen me before. Well, you won't be seeing me again, either, I thought.

A few minutes later, Bai Jianqiu came in with a fair-skinned, long-haired girl in a long skirt with shoulder straps. "Let me introduce you to someone, Gu Lingling. This is Jiafu. Jiafu, this is my girlfriend."

I looked at her. "I've heard him talk about you," I said.

"I've heard him talk about you, too," she replied as she twirled the jade bracelet on her arm.

I had to smile. She was cute, but certainly no pushover. Her reactions were quick. She answered my smile with one of her own, and I liked her immediately.

Their love seemed typical of middle-class boys and girls in any average-sized city—genuine and guileless.

Jia Jia and Bai Jianqiu took seats in the last row, off to the right. I sat down in front of Jianqiu. By myself. It was politics, one of my favourite classes back in Beijing. I hadn't taken a politics course for a very long time and was itching to get started. Deep down I hoped the teacher—a man, I expected—would raise some interesting topics for discussion, and that would give me a chance to display my talents, show them that I really was smart.

Well, class started—the teacher was, in fact, a woman—and instead of a lecture, she told them to review their lesson. What a bummer! I turned and looked behind me. Bai Jianqiu was asleep, head down on his desk. And Jia Jia? He was wrapped up in a book I'd given them called *Introduction to Sex* and wasn't even aware I was looking at him.

I sprawled out on my desktop and began memorizing words in an English textbook. This was so incredible.

After class, I went over to the school snack shop, where I tried a bottle of Kaifeng yoghurt. Not bad, and cheap, only ninety fen. I also bought some chewing gum to give to them. The woman who ran the shop said that Kaifeng residents are all poor, so the cost of living is lower.

When school was out, Bai Jianqiu invited me over to his

place. He and his family lived in a densely populated neigh-bourhood of small apartment buildings. I met his father, a dark, skinny man who greeted me in the local dialect. Jian-qiu's room was neat and clean, with a xylophone in one cor-ner; some of his own paintings and some homemade posters of the band hung on the walls. "I'm going to buy my own bass guitar this year," he said.

He and Gu Lingling liked each other a lot, and goofed around quite a bit.

"I'll give you a jade ornament," she said with a smile, "and you and I can be sisters."

"Sounds too good to be true," I replied.

She took a tiny jade lock out of her purse. "I have a little jade key for this," she said. "They're a set. One for you and one for me. Starting today, you and I are sisters."

"They're real jade," Jianqiu said.

She pulled out a strand of hair to test it. It was real jade, all right.

"See, I told you." Jianqiu smiled proudly.

I spent the rest of the afternoon at Li Zhanwu's apartment, then he took me to see the sights around town. First we went to a music shop, where he told me it was where he used to buy copies of *Music and Video World* and *Punk Age*. It was the only music shop in Kaifeng where you could buy rock maga-zines. They also sold audiotapes and pirated CDs. I did some window-shopping for clothes and checked out a Xinhua Bookshop.

The sun baked down on us. I was wearing a red T-shirt, a black-and-white checked skirt, and red sneakers—dazzling youth. Li Zhanwu took me to a district where there was an abandoned auditorium; we climbed the cement steps to the top and sat down to talk. I bought a beer, and he told me he never drank, but the two of us shared the bottle anyway.

As evening fell, Li Zhanwu said we ought to get something to eat—his treat. At a bustling marketplace we ate some ice cream and had a couple of soft drinks. I said, "Things here are really cheap!"

"That's right," he teased. "So are the workers' wages."

We went back after dark and got the other members of the band to go out on the town. Gu Lingling bought me some red silk thread for the jade lock. She strung it herself and draped it around my neck, and I made a silent vow not to ever take it off.

The next day I told them that I'd be leaving soon. "Where are you going?" Bai Jianqiu asked me.

"Home."

"Where?" He knew what I'd said, but he asked anyway. And I knew I'd rather not answer again, but I did.

"Home."

He just nodded absently. I turned to look at Jia Jia, but he hadn't stopped shooting baskets.

I went to find my mother at a guesthouse near the train station. After our first night in Kaifeng, when she'd stayed at Li Zhanwu's, she insisted on moving into the guesthouse. When I got there, she was drinking water and combing her hair; she seemed happy to me, maybe because she knew we were heading back to Beijing that night, that I no longer insisted on spending a month in Kaifeng, and maybe she was feeling happy that this trip had gone off without incident. Who knows? Whatever the reason, seeing her happy like that made me pretty happy too.

Jianqiu and Li Zhanwu went with us to the train station and watched our train pull away. But before we left, Li Zhanwu took a cross from around his neck and put it around mine.

16 | LONELY HIGH-HEELED SHOES

Back to school.

My absence from school to visit Kaifeng greatly disappointed Teacher Wang. At night, when I walked home along the western section of Third Ring Road, I often ran into her, and it was awkward. When that proved unbearable, I finally made the following entry in my weekly journal:

A hypothesis:
Shall we continue to understand and support one another like good friends, or give one another the silent treatment?
If the former, why don't we pick a time and talk this out? If the latter, then there's nothing I can say except that I'm guilty of a bad decision.

When the journals were returned, I found these lines at the bottom:

You want to talk it out? That's fine if you're willing to open up and speak honestly. I don't feel as if I was deceived as much as I don't think you've treated me as a true friend.

There are simply some things you should talk to me about before you do them.

If you still want to talk, pick a time.

But the mutual esteem Teacher Wang and I had enjoyed was gone forever; we now kept each other at arm's length, not your ordinary student-teacher relationship.

Four students in our class left as a group for another school, one that specialized in teaching English. After completing the seven-year programme, the students graduated with the equivalent of a college degree. The tuition was reputed to be exceptionally high. They were lucky, breaking out of this insane asylum of a school. None of us doubted that any school would be better than ours.

They had escaped. I, on the other hand, the one most desperate to leave, was still there.

That night I had a horrible nightmare.

The whole thing was filled with hopeless love, hopeless yearnings, hopeless flight, hopeless hopes. In the dream someone I've always liked gives one of my young aunts a black liquid. "Don't drink that!" I scream. "Don't drink it!"

That is followed by flight and more flight, running madly, and when I finally awoke, I was overcome by a fear of death, a fear of freezing loneliness and of cold, and the understanding that no matter whether it's life or death, everything is controlled by something unknowable and mysterious.

A few days after returning to Beijing, I went silent, no longer going on and on about SpermOva. When I did speak, I began asking a bunch of childish questions: Do you have any true friends? Do you believe in love? Some of the people shook their heads, some nodded. When they asked me the same questions, I didn't have a clue.

Like the song says: *Take off your lonely high-heeled shoes and walk barefoot on the steps of the world's parks. My dreams are not of Paris, or Tokyo, or New York. My loneliness and I will meet in the quiet and stillness of midnight. . . .*

3

rotten lemons

17 | STARTING OVER

It was June 12. I remember the date because there was a show called "Underground Action" that night, which featured many of my favourite bands. But I didn't have the money or the time to go.

Instead Zhao Ping, the lead singer of the band W, and I had agreed to meet at the Beijing Normal University main gate. He sounded hoarse as hell over the phone, and when we finally met, it turned out that his voice matched him perfectly, travel-weary and worn looking, as if he'd just returned from Xinjiang Province. Before we met, he'd gone to Beijing Normal to size up a prospective mate, and I heard that the minute she laid eyes on him, looking like a bum, she'd refused to come downstairs. He showed up with another boy, who introduced himself as Chi Lei. He was the exact opposite of Zhao Ping, your standard Beijing kid: short hair, a clean denim shirt, almost morbidly serious. As we were crossing the street on our way to The Ark Bookshop, Zhao Ping took my hand, as if it were the most natural thing in the world. His hand was warm, not hot, just warm. When he went with me to buy a bottle of water, I said I'd treat him to a yoghurt. At first he seemed hesitant, but then he smiled and said "Thanks". Later on, I discovered that he didn't have any money. Not just on him, but broke.

I took Zhao Ping home with me, where he sat on the balcony and sang some of the poems he'd written, accompanying himself on my guitar. I took some ice cream out of the freezer, and shared it with him—a spoonful for him, a spoonful for me, with me doing the feeding. He said I had sexy legs. That was good to hear. Li had never once given me a compliment. He'd never said that anything about me was sexy. Zhao Ping kissed me once we were in my room. Nervous, we turned on the light and kept an ear cocked for my parents in the living room.

The next day Zhao Ping invited me over to an apartment he'd rented at Tree Village, which people called Rock 'n' Roll Village. I didn't have anything better to do, so I went. We met at Beijing Normal, then rode our bikes way out to Tree Village together. He took me to his apartment there in the western suburbs, which was really close to my stupid school. A foul-smelling river snaked its way through the area. He showed me his paintings, which were in several folios. One had nothing but green paintings. He called it "The Hell in My Dreams".

Going to bed with him seemed perfectly natural. Like the first time, with Li, I didn't even ask if he had a girlfriend. I hadn't made love in half a year at least, and he hurt me a lot;

I screamed while he was on top of me. He just snickered. "You're not a virgin, are you?" he asked. That got to me.

"Neither are you, so what difference does it make? Your problem is you only took me to bed because you thought I was a virgin. You're too old-fashioned to be in rock 'n' roll."

So I demanded that he get off. He smiled and told me not to be angry, that he was just teasing.

During computer class at school, I typed out Zhao Ping's poem "Little Sister". I liked it better than his long poems and lyrics, which were all filled with either slander or praise. This one was simple, pure, beautiful.

Beneath the vast blue sky
Hand in hand with Little Sister
We come to a rich harvest in the rye field
A carpet of brilliant golden yellow

Little Sister's smiling face is a flower
As she chases sparrows through the furrows
I see cuckoos in the sky
Suanhuang, Suange

Eight hundred li of northern provinces
A plateau of yellow earth
Is my childhood home
And Little Sister's

"I copied out your poem 'Little Sister' in computer class," I said casually as I lay on his simple bed the following Saturday. His eyes sparkled.

"You did?" he replied a little awkwardly.

"Yeah. I really like it, especially the 'Eight hundred li of northern provinces/A plateau of yellow earth . . . ' It's very evocative. What does 'Suanhuang Suange' mean?"

"Those are the names of two kinds of cuckoos back home."

"Did you write that poem for your kid sister?"

"I wrote it for my first love. In Shaanxi we call lovers Little Sisters."

"Oh . . ."

"She's great. She's at Beida now."

Zhao Ping told me a little about his relationship with her and showed me a picture. A cute girl, posing with her head cocked to one side. She was smiling.

"The first time we did it was on a bench by Weiming Lake on the Beida campus. We were real jittery. She was a virgin."

"Were you?"

"Heh heh, yeah, I guess I was." He was grinning happily.

"So why'd you break up?" I was curious.

"Some things happened." Obviously, he didn't want to tell me too much. He got out of bed and put the photo away.

"Ever see her again?"

"Not really."

"Why don't you go look her up at Beida?"

"I wanted to, but her classmates kept me from seeing her. They stopped me from even getting in the gate."

"Why?" That was puzzling, didn't sound quite right.

"Let's change the subject," Zhao Ping said impatiently.

*　*　*

Zhao Ping came to school for me a few days after that. "PK14 is here."

"Honest?" PK14 was a Nanjing band I really wanted to see. "Are you kidding me?"

I wasn't sure I believed him. We jumped on our bikes and sped over to the apartment where Mao Dou, the W drummer, lived. "Come in, Chun Sue, and say hello to your uncles." He ushered me into the room where some young guys sitting on the floor looked up. I nearly jumped out of my skin. PK14 really had come to Beijing! I'd only read about them in magazines, but I recognized Yang Haisong, the lead singer, right off. He was wearing glasses and had on a cartoon T-shirt. He looked like a good-natured guy. I talked briefly with the band members, then found an excuse to slip away. The atmosphere was too much for me to handle.

Outside, I squatted down on the lawn and was plucking blades of grass when a girl came up and squatted down beside me. "Are you a fan of W?" she asked.

At the time I didn't know that this girl was Mao Dou's girlfriend, and I wondered why she wanted to know. The truth is, she wanted to find out why I was hanging around Zhao Ping. She thought that maybe I was a W groupie, and that's why I'd latched on to its lead singer. She was way wrong.

"No, I think W is a pretty ordinary band. I'm not crazy about their music."

"How old are you?" the girl asked me.

I told her, though I didn't really want to. "Going on sixteen."

"You're pretty young to be hanging out with a guy like Zhao Ping. You don't think you'll regret it one day?"

"Who gives a damn? No one can predict how things will turn out." I stood up. She looked at me, but I couldn't tell what she was thinking.

My friend Little Orchid lived nearby, and I decided to go see him, figuring that would be more fun than being in a roomful of strangers. His living room was virtually empty, the bedroom was furnished only with a bed and a dresser. He asked me in, then got back into bed. I'd only been there a few minutes when I heard somebody outside shout "Chun Sue! Chun Sue!" I walked out, and Zhao Ping just looked at me, obviously unhappy, not saying a word. I had no idea why he was so pissed off. "How come you came to see him?" he asked finally.

"Just to talk," I replied nonchalantly.

"Why didn't you tell me?"

I stared at him. "Why should I? We're all friends—you're my friend, so is Little Orchid. . . ." That got to him. He grabbed my arm and started dragging me back to the apartment.

"What the hell do you think you're doing?" I demanded angrily. "Just what the hell do you think you're doing?"

"Let's go eat," was all he said in return.

We walked by the river. It was dusk, and the setting sun's rays lit up the green water. Zhao Ping walked to my left, with the band out in front. I stared at the river, and it looked like an unripe lemon that had already turned rotten. Like me.

"You're pretty high and mighty," someone said in a tone reeking of loathing.

I smiled bitterly, and Zhao put his arm around my waist. "If all this really makes you uncomfortable, you're free to go—go on!" I turned around and started walking, taking my feelings of hopelessness with me, wanting only to jump on my bike and get the hell out of there. But I hadn't taken more than a few steps before Zhao Ping pulled me back. Sighing and keeping his head down, he said, "Hell, let's eat. . . ." I caved in. I was such a wimp. All anyone had to do was be halfway nice to win me over. I was miserable. While we walked, I told him I preferred guys with good bodies, young men who were persistent, honest, passionate, and strong. Either that or men who are open-minded about me. He was neither, he said. I glanced at him. He was right, he was neither of those types. More like a shrunken little man, old before his years, out of step, someone who blows up over nothing. Writing poetry, painting, and playing music. He had every shortcoming an artist can have. He was promiscuous, hardened, full of contradictions, and vain. And still I stayed with him. I was the one who was screwed up.

We walked back together after dinner so I could get my backpack. His room was dark. I walked in first, and he locked the door behind him. "Motherfucker!" I glared at him.

He stared back, and I watched as his face got all twisted. His eyes bored right through me. I wasn't scared at all, I was furious. I stared back, trying to provoke him. "Go on, hit me if you've got the guts!" All I heard was a low, agonizing moan. Then he fell to the floor and began to sob miserably. That was the last thing in the world I expected. With his ragged clothes and ratty hair, he looked like some grubby, whipped animal. I was shocked. I'd expected him to climb all over me or something. But no, he cried until he started to shudder, and he couldn't speak. Finally he looked up at me. "Moth . . . how dare you say things like that about Mother? You don't know what a kind, decent woman she was. I'd rather you kill me than hear things like that about my mother." The mean look in his eyes was gone. All I saw now were helplessness and self-pity. "Lie down and talk with me for a while, Sue." I didn't say anything. Almost as if talking to himself, he went on, "I really loved my mother, she's dead now, she was so good to people, sometimes I think about her and I go a little crazy, I was her only son. . . ."

He started telling me all about his mother, and to hear him, you'd think she was the greatest, most caring mother who'd ever lived. Beautiful, kindhearted, a devoted home-maker who loved her child so much she was willing to sacri-fice her leisure and personal happiness for him. Your typical rural Chinese working mother. When Zhao Ping spoke about how hard she'd worked every day, how she'd refused to buy medicine even when she was sick, and how she'd lacked the strength to fight off her last illness and had passed away, all I could think of was, Where was his father all this time? What was he doing? Taking it easy while he watched his wife waste away? It didn't bother him that his wife was sick and refused to buy medicine to get better? But that's not how Zhao Ping saw it. Or maybe the thought never occurred to him. He said his father was the most decent, most honest peasant in the village and that he was his father's second child and the one he was most proud of.

"My maternal grandmother called my mother her little worker ant, because even as a little girl she'd slaved away without complaining, a model child. Never once in her life did she ask for anything, and she never borrowed a cent, not even for medicine when her health was at risk. She treated everyone with great warmth; she never gossiped about other people, she never lost her temper. The day she passed away, the whole village wept. That night I slept on her grave, and afterward I wrote a poem for her. I called it 'A Stormy Night in May'."

That night we ended up making quiet love, then he took me over to Zhongguan Village, and I rode home alone. On the way my thoughts were all over the place. I knew he wasn't right for me and that this wasn't love. I just didn't know how to break it off.

In the evenings that summer, just before the sun went down, we'd sit on a log in his doorway, looking up at the sky and eating pears. He told me he hoped to put out ten albums, then he'd concentrate on his painting, travelling around the country in the footsteps of his favourite poets. I sat there listening. "Have another, Sue." He handed me the last pear. I took a big bite. They were small pears, and puckery, but he couldn't afford better ones. The sky was bright blue, the weather couldn't have been nicer. I was such a dummy I let myself forget how wrong everything was.

19 | DEMEANING LOVE

When I was nine, I lived with my father in a military camp. My mother and younger brother stayed in the countryside. I craved attention, and spent a lot of time raising hell with the soldiers. They liked me as much as I liked them. One day one of them told me to come with him to his barracks. So I went.

I spent lots of time there anyway. I wore my hair in braids, and the soldiers all called me their "little angel". This time the building was deserted, except for us, and when I sat down on a stool, he took off his pants. He wasn't wearing any underwear. "Like it?" he asked me. He told me to touch it, but I wouldn't, and I could see he was getting edgy. He walked over and shut the door. Then he asked again, "Like it?"

"Like what?" I asked. "Er, no, I don't like it," I corrected myself. I went over and opened the door, and the guy just watched, dreamy-like. He had a real dreamy look in his eyes.

"Are you telling me the guy tried to rape you?" Zhao Ping asked when I told him the story.

No . . . what I wanted to tell him was that after all that time, I could still see the dreamy look in the guy's eyes. I still remembered him. I don't know if that meant I loved the guy or hated him, but he was the bravest man I ever saw. Maybe he should have taken things a step further. But that's all he did, and I still remembered him.

* * *

Sometimes Zhao Ping would wait for me at the gate when school let out, so as soon as my last class was over, I'd smear suntan lotion on my face to make my skin as light as possible. Boys in the class would shout, "Jiafu's putting on suntan lotion again, bet she's got another date!"

We'd keep our distance from one another at the gate, then ride shoulder to shoulder. He'd see me home, then after dinner I'd go looking for him. I'd bring money along so he could get something to eat, or I'd bring him leftovers. He never had any money and was always underfed.

Most of our time together we spent in parks, especially nearby Yuyuantan. Then there was Purple Bamboo Grove, a perfect place to cool off in the summer. Sometimes we'd make love in a secluded corner. But even then I was sometimes thinking it was time to bring things to an end.

"When our band makes its album," Zhao Ping said, "I'll give you ten copies."

The day they made an album was probably a long, long way off.

The reputation of Zhao Ping's band was on the rise, and they'd become the idols of underground rock fans from outside Beijing, who were pretty much out of touch. A newspaper story went so far as to say that "W is a rock band with the potential to create a powerful fan base less than a year after its founding. The band has a powerful style that incorporates a heavy dose of experimentation, reminiscent of Sonic Youth. Their lead singer, Zhao Ping, is what distinguishes W from other bands. Think what The Doors would have been without Jim Morrison. Zhao Ping's penchant for giving up his body as he bounds around the stage is downright shocking. He incorporates poetry into the songs and their incurable melodies drive fans crazy." Rumour had it that even Cui Jian and Pangu's lead singer Aobo were big fans of the group. So at the time, Zhao Ping and his band were trying hard to scrape up the money to cut their first CD.

Still, most music magazines called W an ill-fated, post-noise band with obscure metaphors imbedded in ear-piercing guitar riffs. Zhao Ping sang softly, like the moans of a prisoner in Hell, and the grief and indignation emerging from the songs drove a stake through the listener's heart.

I was just disgusted by the benevolent look in Zhao Ping's eyes and hated things like "Get close to the earth and to the hardworking, simple, plain folk." That and bullshit phrases like "Look after and cleanse your soul."

* * *

Another dirty, filthy Saturday night. I went to see Zhao Ping and watched their rehearsal, until he waved his tattered mess of a hat in the air and proclaimed it was time for dinner. I asked if he had any money, but I knew the answer without having to ask. "We're broke." I told him I didn't even have cab fare home.

"Hell, we're only going for noodles, so don't worry," he said impatiently, his Shaanxi accent heavy as always.

So I went. At a little café at the edge of the village, he ordered a bowl of noodles with tomatoes and eggs. I felt like I was walking on eggshells. What kind of game was this? What was going to happen when it came time to pay? I sat there looking at Zhao Ping's gaunt face, blackened by the sun, and his small, exhausted body, conflict raging in my mind.

When the bill came, Zhao Ping told the waitress he didn't have any money, and that he'd make it up next time. The bowl of noodles cost four RMB, but she let us go.

I decided to take a cab after all. I figured I'd get the money to pay the driver at home. From Rock 'n' Roll Village, beyond Fourth Ring Road all the way to Wanshou Road—was I going to have to explain the steep fare with my tears?

After the driver saw me say good-bye to Zhao Ping, he asked, "He your boyfriend?"

I paused. "No," I finally said. "He's one of the people I was interviewing."

"How old are you?" The cab driver looked back at me.

I stared off into the darkness and tree shadows ahead. "Eighteen."

"Eighteen?" the driver said enviously. "Lucky you. At seventeen or eighteen, you kids are like flowers, blooming happily. No worries, no cares, just onward and upward."

I'd long forgotten what it meant to have no worries, no cares, to be moving onward and upward. I'd strayed too far from those concepts, and didn't know how to return to them. If I was a flower, then I was one of those that bloom in the morning and die the same night. I'd bloomed about as much as I could. But that had been my choice, so I couldn't complain. I held to the existential concept that life is suffering: Do what you want to do, and willingly suffer the consequences. That's how it's supposed to be. There were plenty of things I had to accept responsibility for, because I was indecisive, could never make up my mind. And there were times when I had no idea exactly what I was thinking or what I needed.

* * *

"Is it actually possible you've never doubted any of this?" I asked.

"What do you mean, any of this?"

"Rock music."

Zhao Ping was mumbling as he lay in bed. He said he was tired. Yeah, well, just thinking about being tired tired me out.

I didn't ask any more questions. And we avoided subjects like that from then on. I knew something was wrong with Zhao Ping's rock 'n' roll lifestyle. I can't say what that was, but I couldn't shake the feeling. But we never talked about that, not once, like we were scared to. Besides, what would we wind up with after we'd crossed that threshold? The brutal fact was, there wasn't anything on the other side.

After sleeping in until about noon, we'd get out of bed, then go get some lunch if we had the money. If not, we'd buy stuff at the local market and he'd make lunch. All the time I was with him, I never let myself go hungry. A lot of the time I wondered why I wanted to stay with Zhao Ping. There had to be a reason.

One day I found a letter in Zhao Ping's room while he was out making a phone call. It was from his older sister back home in Shaanxi. I hesitated for only a moment before opening it and beginning to read. She started out by asking how he was, but what followed was absolutely fantastic and scary, enough to make me shudder. What she wrote was nothing like the stuff Zhao Ping usually told me. The letter said his father was responsible for his mother's death, that he'd withheld medicine from her when she was gravely ill. His sister ended by reminding him that he wasn't getting any younger, that it was time for him to get married and settle down. If he didn't know anybody, she told him to come home and she'd find him a wife. That pissed me off. Zhao Ping is with me, so who is she to find him a fucking wife? He's with me now, and that means he's mine! I let the letter slip out of my mind without a second thought.

He called me from somebody's house. Amid the background noise, I could pick out my friend Chi Lei's voice. "Are you calling from Chi Lei's?" He didn't say. "Put him on, I want to talk to him." Chi Lei got on the line.

"Hi, is that you, Chun Sue?" He had a great voice, and we talked for a long time. Things like, he told me where he'd gone to primary school, or I told him there were lots of beauty salons in my neighbourhood. We wondered when we might have a chance to meet and talk face-to-face. I hung up. The phone rang again seconds later.

"Why'd you hang up?" Zhao Ping was nearly shouting. He gave me hell, telling me I had no manners, that all I wanted to do was talk to other people. It sounded like something he'd bring up again, and sure enough, the next time I went over there, he said, "Every one of those guys is out to get you. I'm the only one on your side. Don't trust anyone but me." I shut my eyes and waited to hear what else he had to say.

"You treat everybody so great, but do you know what they think of you?"

"Who cares what other people think of me?"

"You can't shut up. It's okay to talk when you've got something to say, but what did you and Chi Lei talk about that time on the phone? A bunch of shit! And he figured, the way you sounded, you'd be looking him up the next day."

"He didn't think . . ."

"He thought he'd have you the next day and dump you the day after that. What do you think he wants you for?" he said intently, gesturing, like he was in control of everything.

"What business is that of yours, anyway?" I imagined myself saying insolently, then watching his face turn white. The mere thought gave me a rush.

But all I actually did was cry. I curled up in a corner of the bed and listened to him say, "You've got no character. That's the one thing people like you are missing."

"I've got my own ideas," I said. "What's wrong with that?"

Zhao Ping burst out laughing. "Stupid fucking kid!"

I shut my eyes.

"Then why do you want to be with me?"

"Because . . . because you're so cute."

"Just because somebody's cute doesn't mean she's stupid."

"Cute and stupid, same thing."

Like autumn, the meaningless season, or winter with its frigid cold, any feelings we had for each other were long gone.

* * *

"Zhao Ping's nothing special, and there's no reason to try to understand him. He's cheap and he doesn't really care about anything." Chi Lei was on the phone with me one afternoon. He had a soft voice, but what he said was pretty heavy stuff.

I took Chi Lei up on his invitation to go out. He picked me up in a cab, and we went grocery shopping, where he bought lots of my favourite foods, including a couple of ice cream cups. I kept thinking of one of Zhao Ping's poems:

> *"I took the sack with all its human complaints off my shoulder/It was crammed full of sorrow and melancholy/Thunderous curses erupted in the subway aisle/Whose anger rang out like a blacksmith's hammer."*

To me, that poem mirrored Zhao Ping's life. Sorrow and melancholy. Curses and anger. A tragic hero. But in reality, was the author of that poem really a shallow person?

Chi Lei took me to his place. He had two dogs and three cats, and as soon as we stepped in the door, his big hunting dog started barking. That scared me. I've been afraid of dogs ever since I was little, but Chi Lei kept the dog away as I walked inside. The room was carpeted, and a large oil painting hung on the wall. It was a young woman with long black hair, dressed in a red cheongsam.

"Your girlfriend?"

He nodded.

"Is she rich?"

"Yes."

"I've put on weight recently," he said. "The good life, all eating and sleeping and taking it easy. I need to lose a few pounds. You sit here and watch TV while I clean the vegetables outside." Chi Lei turned on the TV, smiled at me, and walked out. I chose one ice cream cup, ate it, and put the other one in the freezer. Chi Lei kept coming in and going back out, busily preparing a meal, which he said he was good at. "Hey, you," he finally called out, "come and eat." He'd made a standard meal, three dishes and a soup. I tasted them all to see if he was as good as he said. Not that it made any difference, since the act of cooking for me made me happy, no matter how it tasted. Afterwards, we sat on the sofa and talked, and he held my hand. . . .

"I'm hopeless. I don't feel safe unless I'm in somebody's arms."

"I don't believe that," he said with a smile.

"I mean it." I quickly forgot the remnants of morality I'd managed to retain in my relationship with Zhao Ping. No big deal, fickle as the clouds and rain. Mired in puberty, melancholy and oversensitive. Do something bad to me, and I guarantee you'll get twice as bad in return.

21 | A LOG AT SUNSET

Zhao Ping called and asked me to go with him to see a music producer, because the band was ready to record an album. He said he'd wait for me at People's University. After I got there, we just sat around for a while. Crowds of people walked past, and a lot of them stared at us. We were an odd couple, that's for sure. I looked like a student, he looked like a wizened old man, down on his luck, quite possibly mental. They probably wondered what I was doing hanging around someone like him, and I had to admit, I wasn't at all sure. And since there didn't seem to be any good reason, I just considered it further proof of my weak character.

We took a bus, but I didn't have any money, and all he had was the two thousand for the record producer. So we stood far apart from one another, and the ticket taker didn't pay us any attention. As the bus was backing up, I suddenly realized I didn't feel like going with him, that I was only there because I'm a goddamned incurable weakling. Or maybe I just have trouble expressing myself. Either way, it was my fault. And consciously or not, he attacked and exploited my irrationality.

So we went looking for the producer. Eventually, we wound up in a village somewhere on the northeast edge of Beijing. A rainfall a few days earlier had turned the roads wet and muddy, which nearly ruined our shoes. It was hot and humid, cicadas chirped endlessly among the trees, and I was dying of thirst. It had taken us three long hours to reach the village, and now I was just standing outside waiting. After about fifteen minutes, Zhao came out and told me the producer wasn't there. He'd had a cup of tea while he was inside. "I'm thirsty, too," I told him.

On the way home, Zhao said he was hungry. I reminded him that he couldn't spend any of the money he'd brought, but he said he was famished and that we should eat something. So we stopped at a little diner for some noodles, the cheapest thing on the menu. He broke a hundred-RMB bill to pay for the food. On the trip back, he refused to buy me a bus ticket, and when the ticket taker came up to us, the damned cheapskate told the guy he didn't have enough money. He took out a crumpled bill he'd got in change from the restaurant and handed it to the guy, who reluctantly gave him a pair of tickets. I sat watching the whole scene coolly, but after we got off the bus, I asked why he hadn't bought tickets, since he had the money.

"You don't understand. For me, paying to ride a bus is a waste."

"I see . . . I see . . ." I was amazed. I just stared at him, not knowing what to say. How can you get mad at an asshole for being an asshole?

Back at People's University, I retrieved my bike. "Fuck! Fuck! Fuck!" was all I could think as I rode off. "Chun Sue!" he called out. I slowed down, stopped, and looked back. "What?"

"Nothing, just be careful on your way home. And thanks for going with me today."

"Oh . . . no big deal," I said, despite what I was thinking. I smiled, and what a cheap smile it was. I turned back and rode on, disgusted with myself. What kept me from telling him what was bugging me? How come I always let somebody else's attitude determine mine? Was Zhao Ping right when he said I had no character?

*　*　*

On another evening we went together to Yuyuantan. We sat by the lake, where the ripples shimmered like scales in the evening breeze. At first we didn't talk. But after a while, he scooted up beside me and talked about his mother. I sat and listened. I knew his thoughts were controlled by circumstances, and that whenever he felt besieged, he thought about his mother; that she was his sole consolation. At such times, and no other, a peaceful, happy look settled on his face. He was a mass of contradictions. He painted, he sang, and he wrote poetry, but none of those could turn him into a normal, ordinary human being.

"What kind of girlfriend will you be looking for down the line?" I asked.

"I'd like to find a foreign woman. Someone I could leave the country with."

"A foreign woman? You, of all people, want to find a foreign woman? You've got to be kidding!" I laughed. So, all along he'd had his heart set on finding a foreigner. What was I then? Spending all this time with him had become a means of self-torture. I hated him. He disgusted me, but that doesn't mean it didn't hurt. And the tears came.

All of a sudden, two blinding beams of light hit us. "Hey! What's going on?"

A pair of beat cops walked up and gave us the once-over. "You should be home at this hour. What are you doing out here?"

"Talking." I stood up.

"Got any identification?"

I glanced at Zhao Ping. "I've got my student ID."

"Let's see it." They kept their flashlights fixed on me.

I fished the ID out of my green backpack and handed it to them. They studied it before handing it back.

"Your dad's in the army?" one of them asked.

"Yes."

"You live on my beat," he said. "What's his name?"

"Please don't ask," I pleaded. "He'd give me hell if he found out." He just looked at me.

"You don't have to stand. Sit down." Zhao Ping tried to pull me down off my feet.

"I want to," I said, with a look at the cop. "If they're standing, I'll stand too."

"Now, that's the right attitude. You're supposed to stand at attention when you're being questioned." The cop turned to Zhao Ping. "Your ID? Where do you live?"

"I've got a temporary residence card," Zhao Ping said as he took it out of his back pocket and handed it over.

"How about a worker's ID?"

"Don't have one . . . I'm a computer software programmer, over at Zhongguan Village."

I nearly laughed out loud. Zhongguan Village? Him? A software programmer?

"You related?"

"She's my kid sister," Zhao Ping said.

"So what are you doing out here this late?" the policeman repeated.

"Just talking."

"Go on, now. It's too late to be hanging around here. We thought you might be part of that Falun Gong cult." They handed back Zhao Ping's temporary residence card and walked off.

"Let's go," I said. I could see he was unhappy about something.

"Why didn't you sit when I told you to?" he asked. "You're supposed to look out for me when there are cops around."

I didn't say anything, just looked at him. A rebel like him, and he needed a girl to look out for him?

I was liking him less and less all the time. He was always broke, his clothes were torn and dirty, like some degenerate. Just looking at him gave me a headache. Especially since he never once thought about how I felt. I'd had all of him I could take. And still I agonized over the situation for a while before making up my mind.

Finally one weekend he "summoned" me, but I didn't go. He started phoning me, over and over, and I always found an excuse not to take the call. After a while, whenever he called, he screamed and cursed, but I treated him like I would a stranger, and slammed down the phone. Then he just sort of disappeared. All I ever heard after that were a bunch of jokes about him or his name on an occasional rock music programme.

We'd been together about six months, from early summer to late fall. By the time the weather started turning cold, we were over. And just like the time before, I felt like a weight had been lifted off me. The one thing I had learned, however, was just how tough these musicians' lives were, that there was no one to help them and no one to worry about them. So even then, I knew how this would all turn out.

4

you're lost little girl

Zhao Ping phoned me again and asked me to come and see him. "We were terrific together, weren't we?" he whined over the phone. "Come over this Saturday. I've missed you." I was unmoved. His dark face, the wrinkles, his down-and-out look, and his moodiness—bummed out one minute, ecstatic the next—made me lose my appetite. Maybe, I was thinking, I ought to make him give up once and for all.

We agreed to meet at the fork in the road at Rock 'n' Roll Village at three in the afternoon the next Saturday. I wanted to bring this to an end, including his interminable phone calls. I swore I'd never again fall into the trap of a bad relationship.

I spotted him way off at the village entrance waiting for

me. He grinned when he saw me ride up on my bike. I braked to a stop beside him. "Come on over to my place." He grabbed my handlebars and started pushing my bike.

"No," I said. "I came here for one reason. I have one thing to say, then I'm leaving. Don't try to stop me. Zhao Ping, it's over between you and me."

"Come on, let's go to my place."

"I said no. Stop pulling me! What do you think you're doing? Let go!" I hit his hand. I was getting really mad.

"My place."

"I said no. I'm going home. Get out of my way."

"My place."

Some people had got off their bikes and were watching us. I was pissed, and I was getting worried. With his hand still on the handlebars, Zhao Ping dragged me and my bike over to the riverbank across the way. I resisted as much as I could, but things were clearly getting out of hand. It was starting to resemble a wrestling match. I was overcome by how sad it all was.

"Come to my place, okay?" Zhao Ping said in a softer tone.

"No."

We sat down on a boulder by the filthy river, which had nearly iced over.

"Let's just talk," I said.

"Then come to my place after we've talked, okay? We'll go out for lunch."

"No, I'm not going."

Zhao Ping put his arm around me. I shrugged it off. He put it back, I shrugged it off again.

"Come over for a while. I won't touch you. I want to show you some paintings I finished over the past few days. I think they're some of the best I've ever done. Come take a look."

"I'm not going."

"God, you're just like my first girlfriend. Toward the end, she refused to come over too." He buried his chin in his chest and mumbled, mixed with what sounded like sobs.

I sat silently looking out at the river, feeling that he, and for that matter, I, were a couple of jokes.

"You don't much like me, anyway," I said.

"Who says so? My life's been miserable lately, I'm sick, there might be something wrong with my lungs. . . ."

"Then get more sleep. . . ."

"I can't. . . ." He glared at me. "Are you trying to get under my skin? I can't sleep, I just can't. . . ."

"I'm sorry."

"Weren't you scared just now I might shove you into the river?" He turned to look at me.

"I've always thought you were capable of something like that," I said with a wry smile.

"Ha!" He laughed.

"I'm going home now, okay? Maybe we'll meet again someday."

"Do you still love me?" Zhao Ping asked out of the blue. I didn't expect that. In all this time we'd never talked about loving or not loving.

"Why do you ask?"

"You don't love me."

"Who says?"

"No, you're not at all concerned about me."

It was true.

"I'm going."

I'd barely made it back home when the phone rang, and I knew it had to be Zhao Ping. Before my mother could pick up the phone, I shouted, "If it's for me, I'm not home!" Just as I thought, a couple of seconds later, I heard her say, "Oh, she's not home. . . ." It didn't take long for the phone to ring again. Zhao Ping must have known that I'd made it home by then. What did he want to say now? What the hell kind of game was he playing? By the nth time he called, my patience had run out. "Ma, I'll get it the next time," I shouted.

"Hello, is that you, Zhao Ping? I made it home all right. What's up?"

"Nothing. I just wanted to hear your voice."

"Really? Well, now you can get some rest," I said with forced tenderness.

"Any chance you could be a sort of kid sister to me? That way we could see each other often."

"Yeah, I can do that."

"That's great."

"Yeah . . . well, take it easy."

I hung up the phone, hoping the end would play itself out quickly.

Zhao Ping started calling any time he felt like it. If I didn't pick up the phone, he'd keep at it until I did. It reached the point that as soon as he heard my voice, he'd just start cursing. I ended up hating him more than I thought possible, and at the same time hated myself for not breaking up with him sooner. I should have figured out what he was like at the very beginning, and ended it then and there. Finally he phoned, and before he had a chance to say anything, I shouted, "You motherfucker, get the fuck out of my life!" That was the last I ever heard of him.

The magazine *I Love Rock 'n' Roll* had a line, "I'm gonna skin rock 'n' roll," and that's what I wanted to do to Zhao Ping, skin his rock 'n' roll exterior and show him for who he really was. He might have fooled others, but I knew all about him. He was born in Xianyang, Shaanxi, in 1974; in 1988 he wrote some "Ah, my ideals have gone far away, but I follow their footsteps" poetry that was published in the *High School Student Literary Daily*; in 1994 he came to Beijing, after spending time in Xinjiang, Yunnan, and Nanjing. In December 1998 he organized the band W. A strange name for a band. His favourite Chinese punk band was Pangu; he turned up his nose at most of the Beijing punk bands. He lived in a rented apartment in Beijing's western suburbs, paying a monthly rent of 140 RMB. He got out of bed in the morning, boiled some water, and began writing poetry. He was always broke, he owed four months' back rent, he went to recording studios on an empty stomach, scrounging what he could, he owed for phone calls and stuffed buns at East Beiwang, he was frail and always sick with something, managing to hit his best friends up for money to buy the medicine he needed. I knew that hidden beneath his halo of fame and wealth was the son of a peasant.

23 | TWO WORLDS

Bai Jianqiu from SpermOva phoned to tell me that he and Jia Jia were coming to Beijing in a week or so. They wanted to see me and, while they were at it, pick up some punched CDs to sell back home.

I was in class the morning they arrived. School authorities had clamped down on absences lately, so I left the guys a note on the table at home, told my mother they were coming, and went to school.

They were waiting for me when I got home that afternoon. Bai Jianqiu was playing my xylophone. They hadn't changed a bit. Jianqiu was wearing a yellow shirt, Jia Jia looked a little spaced out. My mother said she'd had a soldier take them to see the Forbidden City and arranged for them to spend the night in a navy officer's guesthouse nearby.

"Jiafu, will you take us to see a show while we're here?"

"Sure." I took a copy of *Modern Skies* out of my dresser. "There's a show tomorrow night at Club 17. Wooden Horse and some other band will be playing. We can go to that."

"Great."

That night I took them to the guesthouse, then walked home alone.

The next night we took the subway to a bar in Sanlitun. We sat at a rear table, drinking and talking. A foreign guy sat alone at the table in front of ours. He was wearing black and hardly moved, except once in a while he stood up to take a picture, then quietly sat back down and took a couple of swigs of beer. He had a nice back, with gentle curves under his black shirt. His body gave off a sort of elegance I liked a lot. Later on I'd understand that that was a special quality of shy people.

"That foreigner looks interesting," I said.

"Got the nerve to go up and talk to him?" Jia Jia asked.

"Me? No way. Besides, talk about what? My English is so bad it's beyond hope."

"Who cares?" Bai said to egg me on. "Go on, go talk to him. I'll bet he's bored, sitting there all alone. Go on, it's no big deal."

"Nah," I said with a smile. "Maybe later."

But I kept looking at him. I watched as he ordered another beer, and when the girl brought it over, he said, "Thank you."

"Maybe I will, after all," I said.

"Go ahead. We'll wait for you here."

I finished off my ice cream, stood up, and walked up to the guy. "Excuse me," I said. "You want talk somebody?"

"Absolutely," he replied. The music was so loud he gestured that we go outside to talk. I winked at Jia Jia and Bai Jianqiu and walked out with the guy.

Outside there was a little girl selling flowers and some other kids begging for money. I smiled, he shrugged his shoulders. Suddenly I realized that he'd come out wearing only a black T-shirt and was hugging himself in the cold, so I dragged him into a little sundries shop to get warm. A girl was talking on a mobile phone, nearly shouting, in English. Maybe the bar had been too noisy for her too, so she'd come here to make a phone call.

"Where you from?" I asked in English.

"Finland, in Northern Europe."

He repeated himself over and over, but I didn't get what he said. "What?"

The girl on the mobile, impatient, said in Chinese, "Finland, you know, Fen-lan, in Northern Europe."

Her rebuff upset me. She probably thought I was trying to hook up with this foreigner with my awful English.

"Teenager . . ." That's probably what she was thinking.

Finally, we borrowed a pen and paper from the shop clerk to communicate by writing. It was easier than trying to talk. Our accents diluted the few words I thought I knew in English.

He wrote his name—Janne—and said he was visiting Beijing. He was staying at the Jinglun Hotel until Friday. Exactly one week. We wrote back and forth for a while. Janne gave me the phone number of his hotel room, I gave him my home number.

We went back to the bar and continued our conversation. The bands had stopped playing by then, so after a while Janne, Jia Jia, Bai Jianqiu, and I got up and left. I introduced Janne around, "These are my two friends." He smiled at them. Janne and I walked ahead, leaving Jia and Bai behind. I was feeling great. After we'd walked a while, Jia and Bai caught up to us. "You guys keep talking. We're going to grab a cab and head home."

"Okay," I said. I waved at them as they got into the cab.

"I like your friends," Janne said.

"Yeah, they're good guys. They love rock 'n' roll."

Janne's eyes were a gentle gray, with silvery, glassy sparkles. He had straight brown hair. In Finnish, his name was pronounced Yanne, but when I first met him I called him Jian.

He was leaving in a week, so what did I want? If it was possible, what I wanted was a kiss. That's all.

I was a second-year high school student, and before I knew it, my youth would be over. I hated loneliness, and yet I was lonely.

* * *

Janne didn't know a word of Chinese, and my knowledge of English was woefully inadequate. When we talked, it was mostly on paper. That night we walked all the way up to where we could see the outline of the Jinglun Hotel. "Are you busy tomorrow?" he asked as we were saying good-bye. "Let's meet at the same place, seven-thirty."

I found Finland on a map. It was in Northern Europe. It must be freezing in the winter.

It took an hour on the subway to get to Club 17, where we'd agreed to meet. At 7:30, Janne still hadn't shown. I bought a sandwich and ate it while I waited. Ten minutes till eight, and still no sign of Janne, but I decided to wait a little longer. I didn't want to be disappointed on such a beautiful night.

He showed up just before eight. "Sorry," he said.

"It's okay," I said.

We went into the bar, where we talked for a while. I asked him when he might come back to Beijing; he said maybe next August, but there was no guarantee. He told me, "I don't want you to be sad because I'm leaving," and I recall saying, "Never mind."

As we were leaving the bar, Janne insisted on picking up the tab. We walked out into the street. Cars were lined up, headlights glaring. That's Beijing in the winter. Walking into the wind is like hitting a wall.

Like the night before, Janne and I just walked, which was fine with me, since I was trying to stretch the time out as much as I could. I really wanted to be with him, I was so lonely.

"Want to sit here for a while?" he asked by a bench beneath the overpass.

We chatted about nothing in particular, but the language barrier was too great to keep the conversation going. He spoke very fast, in English, and even though I didn't understand all the words, I got the gist of what he was saying by his facial expressions. He said that if we had sex it would be impossible to be ordinary friends afterwards.

God, no, that's not what I wanted.

It's not.

Tears flashed in my eyes. I was angry and contemptuous of myself at the same time. But that's how it was, and there was nothing I could do about it. Two people from different countries, speaking different languages, yearnings separated by time and space.

*   *   *

Janne and I made a date for the next night, our third. When the phone rang, I sprang for it—didn't want my mother or father to get this one. Janne asked what time we were meeting tonight. "Eight-thirty," I said.

My folks were in the living room playing mahjong with friends. At about 7:30, after I'd got myself ready to go out, my father abruptly stopped me.

"Where do you think you're going at this hour? You're staying home!"

"What? But I've got something to do."

"I don't care. It's too late to be going out."

"Honest, I've got something to do." Panic was setting in. I watched the clock as the time I was supposed to meet Janne crept closer.

"I can't reason with her," my father said to his guests. "She thinks she can do whatever she pleases. If I catch her going out tonight, I'll break her legs!"

That started the tears flowing. "You'd do that? How did I wind up with a father like you?"

"How did I wind up with a daughter like you?"

"I'm going out!"

"Just see if you can get through that door!" he said triumphantly, and I knew I had no choice. By the time I had managed to sneak past him, jumped in a taxi to the subway station, taken the subway, and run panting up to the bar entrance, it was already 10:20. Janne wasn't there. Not a trace. All that for nothing. I decided to call his room, thinking maybe he'd already gone back there. I needed to explain what had happened, that it wasn't my fault. . . .

"Hello!" It was a foreign girl.

I told her I was looking for Janne.

"He's not here," she said. "He went out. I'm his sister. Want to leave a message?"

"No, thanks." I hung up, happy that he hadn't gone back to the hotel. But where was he? I decided to wait until I could call his sister again and learn that he was back in the hotel asleep.

About forty minutes later I saw him. I was thrilled. He didn't look happy.

"Sorry I'm late."

"It's all right, last time it was me." That's all he said, and there was no warmth in his reply.

His indifference, not even asking why I was late, really bummed me out.

This time, instead of going into Club 17, we just walked aimlessly. Janne had a stern look on his face, and I wondered if, during the two hours I was late in getting there, he'd changed his mind about me.

We walked over to Sunlitun Bar Street, and when a little girl tried to sell him a rose, he waved her off impatiently.

He ordered a beer for himself and asked me, "What'll you have?"

The racket all around us was deafening.

"Nothing for me," I said. I didn't have enough to buy any of the drinks on the menu.

He looked at me, sort of embarrassed, before turning back and concentrating on his beer.

We couldn't have felt more uncomfortable, and things were quickly going from bad to worse.

I handed him the notepad, on which I'd asked him what he was thinking.

"Nothing."

"Then what do you want to write to me?"

"Sorry, I don't understand. Maybe I've got nothing to say right now, sorry."

"I get the picture. I've wasted your time. If I've wasted your time, I'll leave and go home."

"No, that's not what I mean."

On the notepad he wrote:

"I'm sorry. I have to go, and I think you'd better go home too. It's been so nice to be with you, but after all, we live in different countries, speak different languages, so don't miss me. You have your own happy life."

My happy life? Bullshit! You have no idea how bad it is for us. There's a million miles between us.

"I'm so sorry . . ."

"No problem!" I ran out of the bar, my mouth dry and cottony. It was all wrong.

Janne anxiously followed and said lots of things to me, none of which I understood. It's hard enough for Chinese to connect with other Chinese, since one sentence can mean several things, and different tones and nuanced words can produce radically different effects until you don't know whether someone is praising you or insulting you. I was caught up in my thoughts and couldn't stop the tears from flowing. Just the idea that this foreigner might see what a joke I was turned the faucet on.

"Don't hate me," he said.

"Shut up!" I shot back.

He wrote a line from a Doors song on the notepad:

You're lost little girl.

I stepped onto the overpass and stared down at the cars streaming below. I told him to go ahead without me, I wanted to be alone. After watching him climb into a taxi, I walked over to Chang'an Avenue to catch a late-night bus. I only had two RMB on me.

Janne didn't call Thursday night. When I went to school Friday morning, his plane had already left China.

24 | TRICKING THE MASSES

My old friend Ziyu wrote to say that the Scottish plains were no longer as pretty as they'd been in the summer. He was waiting for the winter, when the sun's bright rays would light them up again. Then no matter where you stood, you forgot all kinds of things.

Bright sun's rays, a blue sky, robust people out on the streets, cars threading their way up one side and down the other.

But I was getting more depressed by the day.

School, any school, was more than I could take. Not a day went by that I was not unhappy there. I didn't want stupid people trying to get inside my head. I didn't want to do any loudspeaker calisthenics or shit like that. I got only dirty looks from the teachers, and I was fed up with all of them. Except, maybe, the one who taught law. He seemed okay. I wanted to know what sign he was born under, but every time I asked him, he kept me guessing.

Nietzsche once said: I'd rather seek nothingness than seek nothing.

One of the girls in class leisurely cruised along in full command of her youthful, radiant, magnificent, splashy beauty.

What incredible shame I felt.

One of the other girls always came out on top on every exam.

I had no place to hide.

*   *   *

I often puzzled over Du Yuan's state of mind. How could she spend her days in school never late never leaving early always smiling hard at work? Every student at West X High hated the school with every bone in their body. Du Yuan herself often complained, calling Director Wang, who was in charge of the student association, a "damned old hag" behind her back. So how was she able to hold her emotions in check? Her status flourished, as she rose to the position of director of the arts and letters society. Full of energy, she was always calling a meeting to investigate something or other. Opportunities for her were all over the place.

Maybe she was also puzzled about my state of mind. Wondering why I was incapable of holding my emotions in check. Why was I so intent on dropping out of school? What in the world was I thinking?

I know that sometimes it's better for others to point the way for you than to make your own choices. There's one road to take, so you take it. Keeps regrets to a minimum. But the way chosen for me was not for me.

Freedom freedom freedom freedom. Freedom to eat, freedom to sleep, freedom to speak, freedom to sing, freedom to make money, freedom to turn on the lights, freedom to kill yourself, freedom to read, freedom to listen to music, freedom to make love, freedom to give up, freedom to go home, freedom to quit school, freedom to run away, freedom to spend money, freedom to cry, freedom to curse someone, freedom to leave home, freedom to speak, freedom to make choices, freedom freedom freedom freedom, freedom freedom freedom freedom; if you're not free, how can you talk about freedom?

I demanded to be allowed to quit school. My parents took me to see a shrink, mainly for the benefit of my teachers and the school. It snowed that day—I think it was January 3 or 4, I can't be sure. We were driven by a soldier from my father's unit to a distant military hospital, way out in the suburbs. It took more than an hour to get there from our house. Sort of like a family outing. The snow was beautiful.

We went into a room on the fourth floor. A sign at the door said "Psychiatric Ward", which I thought was hilarious. A doctor sitting at a large desk coldly asked, "What's your name?" She was neither sweet nor warm.

"Why should I tell you?" I said.

"Why do you think you're here? I asked you your name, so let's get on with it."

She stopped writing and looked straight at me. "You think you're being rebellious, right?"

"I'm sitting here only to flatter you," I said.

Her mouth fell open in shock. Then she assumed the look of someone whose skin was too thick to be bothered. "Is that so?" She sounded thoughtful. This was a woman who could have me declared a lunatic, a raving lunatic. Instead, it was decided that when this semester ended, I'd never have to go back to school. I laughed until I cried.

On the way home we stopped at a restaurant for a wonderful hot-pot meal. Like some sort of celebration. That gave me a rush, but only for a second, since I realized there was nothing to celebrate. How likely was it that my parents were actually celebrating the early end of my schooling? We were back on the road at four or five o'clock, just as schools were letting out. The sidewalks were alive with students from middle school through college, some in uniform, some not, all innocent and spirited, and I noted how their cheerful figures stood in stark contrast to the blanket of pure white snow.

And that's how it happened. The next morning I didn't have to get up at six o'clock, I didn't have to worry about being late, I didn't have to participate in loudspeaker calisthenics, I didn't have to queue up in the cafeteria to get lunch, I didn't have to take any more tests, or attend meetings, or log on to the computer, or . . .

It all came to an end.

26 | RUN WILD AND SILENT

It took all the beautiful things along with it
I like winter winds
Telling me you need to be strong

Now I've left
I've already left
Leaving behind wailing and weeping

Go ahead, regret it
I'm gone

During the winter I took a break from school, I was offered a job with a magazine. Their offices were located in a large military compound near Five Pines; I'd been there before, but just for kicks. Sometimes I'd go over after lunch, with the afternoon sun shining down on the statue of the Great Man, exuding an aura of tolerance and warmth. The cozy, indolent atmosphere there was just what I wanted.

The office lighting was bright but warm. Everyone had a cubicle, and I wondered when I'd have one of my own. Some of the time the office was swarming with people, at other times it was nearly deserted. I usually sat at the farthest desk on the left, just spacing out. I didn't know what they thought of me. They had plenty of money and lots of experience; they could take friends out to dinner, they wore nice perfume and cologne, their voices were soft and gentle. And I was infatuated with them. I thought, I like you people, which is why I'm able to come across as liking you. I may be nothing but a headstrong kid, but that's fine with me.

Y and Z were friends of mine who'd studied in England. Y, who was no longer a young man, was a photography nut and a soccer fanatic. Girls didn't interest him much. He wore his hair long, and had the young eyes of a colt. Z was several years younger than Y, and I often sat in the office watching him surf the net and carry on muted phone conversations with girls in English. Time and again I watched him talk on the phone in his soft, sweet-sounding English, and felt like clapping my hands over my ears so I wouldn't have to listen to a language I didn't understand.

Spring seemed to pop up out of nowhere. Y and Z started getting really busy, spending more and more time out on interviews, and I seldom saw them in the office. I knew I'd have to leave this place sooner or later, and my infatuation with them would fade away, and that made me sad. Knowing this was something I had no control over made me even sadder.

I sat for long hours at my desk, not doing a thing. Sometimes I'd bring a bouquet of flowers in with me and place them in a vase I'd made out of a two-litre Sprite bottle.

Sunlight streamed in through the windows, which were opened slightly for ventilation. Everyone was busy, no one had any time for me. I felt my youth gently slipping away in that atmosphere, in that large space, in that sunlight.

Finally, one day, I looked around the deserted room, and I thought I'd go crazy. My desk and chair opened their mouths wide to swallow me up. I felt totally unwelcome there. As I think back to that time, I can see that I was slowly losing my mind. Youth is nothing but an age, and they didn't need anyone else's age to remind them of the fact that they'd got old. They didn't need a compressed age, a new open wound.

I went looking for Y and Z at their dorm. Z was there. He told me Y was out taking pictures.

We sat in the common room with the TV on, and I looked at Z out of the corner of my eye as I flipped through a magazine. He was talking on the phone in a low, soft voice, laughing every once in a while, gentle yet sort of shady sounding. From time to time he'd interrupt the conversation with a long, unbroken stream of English, as easy on the ears as a rippling brook. What arrogance.

I walked into the bedroom he shared with Y, saw a bottle of CK cologne, and breathed in the seductive fragrance. All of a sudden, and to my astonishment, Z turned nasty.

"When are you going home? It's almost ten, and I have to go to work tomorrow. I need my sleep."

I didn't know what to say, and in that brief moment,

despair grabbed hold of me. The world was every bit as cruel as people said. It was a struggle, but I walked up and laid my hand on his shoulder. He pulled back. What I really wanted was to sit in his lap, but he stopped me. "Have you been hurt in the past?" he asked with a studied look in his eyes.

"What?" I felt like laughing.

With a sombre look, he said, "You lack sincerity."

I lowered my head. Okay, fine, I lack sincerity. Then . . . screw him. I said I was leaving, and he got up to see me out. At the door he grinned and said, "You little hooligan . . . you're a wild one, all right, the *new* new generation!"

With one last look at him, I ran off, feeling something like sticky blood flooding my brain. I could hear it sloshing around in there as I ran. Faster, faster. What kind of world is this? The wind cut through my pants and into my chest like a knife. I ran like crazy, without making a sound.

5

the abyss of love river

27 | DEAD BUTTERFLIES

Another winter had passed, as cold as all the others. Fourteen years old, fifteen . . . and now it was spring, the time for sandstorms.

That afternoon I decided to go to The Ark Bookshop, where a young guy called Boiled Water worked. When I got there, I saw he was wearing a black Nine Inch Nails T-shirt. He looked smaller than before because he'd cut his hair really short.

"Hey, look who's here," Boiled Water announced as he threw his arms out in an exaggerated greeting. Some of the customers looked up from their books, and a guy I'd recently interviewed, named Jesse, the lead singer in a band, walked over. He was still wearing black-rimmed glasses and a pair of combat boots spray-painted yellow.

He asked how I was coming along on the interview, and I told him it was just about done. Then I returned a Dead Butterflies demo tape I'd borrowed from him.

"How'd you like it?" he asked.

"It was okay," I said. "There were a couple of pretty good cuts on the B side."

"Oh?" He gave me a condescending grin. "Technically, they stink. I couldn't finish it. The opening bars of the first song turned me off. Fuck. If they can put out a demo tape, anybody can."

I ignored him. In the Beijing underground rock scene, everybody hated everybody else.

"It's just the two of them, right?" I said.

"Yeah, no bass."

I popped open the case to look at the liner notes.

Dead Butterflies
Guitar/Lead Singer: G
Drums: LCNTC

The notes gave G's pager number. They both used English "names", a sort of secret code I couldn't break. So, half serious, I called G's pager, wanting to see what kind of guy he was. The phone rang a few minutes later. Boiled Water answered: "Hello, The Ark." He teased the caller, telling him there was someone there who kind of liked their music. I was walking around the shop, which sold lots of cutting-edge music books and magazines, despite its size—no more than a few dozen square feet. Outside, bands put up posters for performances or audition notices for musicians, while half of one of the interior walls was filled with CDs—some selling for 15 RMB, others for 150 RMB—and demo tapes for several bands from Beijing and elsewhere. At the counter you could buy T-shirts, decals, and magazines from Europe and the United States. I picked up some free copies of *Beijing Scene*, *Fun in Beijing*, and a *Reader's Guide* that was lying there. Then I poured myself a cup of water, feeling more and more at home. Boiled Water was kept busy answering the phone. At first, he was conscientious and respectful, bowing slightly as he said, "Thank you for calling The Ark Bookshop." Sometimes it was a customer calling to see if a book had arrived, but often it was one of his friends, and he'd giggle or give whoever it was hell, all in good fun. Back when Boiled Water started working there, he'd just moved to Beijing, and was having a rough time, since his family had stayed behind in a village in Jiaodong. But life was better now. By hanging out in the bookshop, he'd met lots of people, mostly musicians, some of whom became his friends. With nothing better to do, they'd drop by the bookshop to kill time, get a bite to eat, whatever. Their conversations often went like this:

"How's it going?"

"No good. Nothing to do. Went to some shows, exhausting. No more for me. A waste of time. No kidding, I'm not meant to live in this world."

Or: "I'd die for the poet Haizi!"

"I'm going to lie down on the tracks, just like he did."

Stuff like that.

* * *

I sat there caught up in my thoughts, drifting into a mood of weird apathy. Time slipped by. A wind rose up outside, blanketing Beijing with yellow sand. Late March, Beijing was besieged with its annual sandstorms. But we sat comfortably inside, ignoring, for the moment at least, the rotten weather outside and all the things that kept us in a funk. I didn't really care much about time, since time was all I had, anyway. After a half hour or so, G showed up at the bookshop.

G said the first time he saw me I didn't make much of an impression on him, except for the green hair. Another punk chick, was what he thought. He assumed I was Jesse's girlfriend. When he saw Jesse, he asked him what he thought of the demo, and Jesse said he hadn't really listened to it. Then they talked a while about putting on shows. I heard G ask Jesse to help him line up a show, but Jesse said it wouldn't work without a bass. Their conversation ended just as I walked up.

"Are you the lead singer of Dead Butterflies?" I asked.

"Yes."

"What are you looking for in a bass player?"

He looked hard at me. "Nothing special, just someone who shares our ideals."

"How about me?" I said.

That's how I got to know G.

Later that day he took me to meet our drummer, a senior at a nearby high school. We rode there on our bikes, him in his funny-looking yellow-rimmed dark glasses, zigzagging our way over to Number Three Railway High. The school had an old classroom building and a huge athletic ground, where some kids were playing soccer. It was late March, almost

April, and the boys had already changed into short-sleeved white soccer shirts. The school had a distinct grassy smell. Some of the kids stared at us, and I shoved my hands in my pockets.

We never did find the drummer. He'd gone home right after school. Not long after that, we said good-bye on Chang'an Avenue, and I told G I'd call him soon.

The next day I lost my address book. I looked everywhere for it, and while I was looking, I found a slip of paper with G's phone number. I dialled it, and he picked up after a couple of rings. "Hello, is this G?"

"Yes, it is." He was responding to a young female voice. "I'm the only one who uses this phone, so if someone answers, it's got to be me. If no one answers, I'm not home."

"Um. This is Chun Sue, I'm the . . ."

"How're you doin'?"

At first it was kind of awkward, but nice. We talked for a while, and he said he'd been waiting all day for me to call. Embarrassed, I told him I couldn't find my address book. I was always like that, losing things right and left.

28 | GLASS DOLL

Vanished like a dream
I see myself in your eyes
Vanished like a dream, I lose my way in the dream
No matter how hard I look, I can't find it
My dream flies away, all a blur
In my confused, chaotic dream I stand naked

In the heart-shaped box of my dream I run madly
The sky grows dark and misty, I feel strangely frightened
The glass stairs ahead
Are they completely shattered?
My completely shattered heart
Has vanished like a dream

—A poem by Glass

Early morning, I was dreaming when the phone rang. A voice I didn't recognize said, "Hello, is this the number for Chun Sue?"

"That's me."

"I'm the drummer for Dead Butterflies. G gave me your number. He and I are going over to The Ark this afternoon. Want to join us?"

"Sure," I said. "Are you at school now? I hear people talking."

"We're between classes. I'm at the student shop," he answered.

I said, "Say something passionate to me."

That was greeted by silence, then, "Okay. I love you, come quickly."

I laughed. "Great. See you this afternoon—Oh, I forgot. What's your name?"

"Glass."

After we hung up, I washed my face and checked the time: 10:30.

I tried to imagine what he'd look like. At his school the other day, I'd had a wet feeling when we went looking for him. I hoped he had short hair and was a little spacey, a boy who danced behind his own fantasy, and who wore clean white T-shirts with turndown collars.

He and G were already at The Ark when I got there that afternoon. He was exactly as I'd pictured.

"Hi, Chun Sue," he said. "You can call me Glass, since that's what everybody at school calls me. They all say I'm gay." He had a Japanese face, and his eyes were transparent like real glass. His hair was short but not bristly, and he was wearing clean sapphire-blue jeans and a long-sleeved pullover.

We hung out in the bookshop for about an hour. They smoked some cigarettes. Glass said he was a high school senior. He wasn't very talkative. Most of the time, he and G just looked at each other, and I had a funny feeling as I watched them that this was no ordinary friendship. Boiled Water came over several times with a smart-ass comment and then sat down beside me, looking uncomfortable. To be friendly, Glass massaged my ankles, a silent display of understanding.

When it turned dark outside, we rode over to Tiananmen Square, where Glass said good-bye and went home.

"Do you think Glass likes me?" I asked anxiously.

G shot a glance at me. "Sure he does," he said, surprised by my question. To put me at ease, he said that's what the guy was like, quiet and withdrawn. That would change as we got to know each other better.

I phoned the musician Li Yan, who said he'd lend me a bass guitar and that I could pick it up on Sunday, and G and I agreed to meet at Parkson Mall beforehand. He was wearing a freaky white jacket on which he'd drawn some anarchist symbols. When we got to Li Yan's place, lots of people were there, including all the members of Li Yan's band. "This is a friend of mine, G," I announced. Li Yan spotted the keyboard slung over G's back. "You in a band too?" he asked, obviously interested. G told him he had a band, that he was in his first year of high school, stuff like that.

*   *   *

A few days later I took G to a bar where Li Yan and his group were playing. At first, G and I took separate chairs and sat there staring at each other, but then I went over and sat in his lap, and he put his arms around me. During the break, the band asked us if we were boyfriend and girlfriend, and warned G that if he didn't treat me right, he'd answer to them. We laughed and we talked, feeling kind of touchy. At one point, I glanced at the guitarist, Xiaohai, who sat with his head down, the overhead lights creating delicate shadows on his face. When he saw that I was looking at him, he smiled.

Up on the stage, he kept his head down while he played the guitar, and I began to fidget in G's lap. I wanted to ask Xiaohai, What are you thinking about? Do you want me? Why don't you show it? Why hold back? I had the feeling that I really cared for him, enough that I didn't want to hurt him. I struggled with mixed feelings of apprehension and desire. When Xiaohai went up to the bar for some mineral water, I walked up next to him.

*   *   *

I felt as if I'd known Xiaohai for a very long time; his face was beautiful but blurry, like it was submerged in water. His actions were gentle, never exaggerated, the ambiguous elegance of a European gentleman. It's a really hard feeling to put into words; I felt that Xiaohai was concerned about me but never in an intimate way, that there was something in his personality that made him want to maintain a distance between him and everybody else. He had the quality of ice mixed with water; though cold, he was gentle. Sometimes I felt like getting close to him, like to a really close friend, or a sensitive, sympathetic doctor. I wanted him, I worshipped him, but there was always something about him that pushed me away. He never expressed any true feelings for me; if he had, I'd have fallen passionately in love with him.

If we stayed too late at a bar, he'd often invite me to spend the night at his place, a big three-bedroom apartment in the building where his parents lived, though they only occasionally came downstairs, which gave the place an almost dizzying sense of freedom. Sometimes I slept in the master bedroom, and sometimes I slept on the single bed in his room, where bubbles from the goldfish popped above the surface of their bowl and the air conditioner hummed sweetly. "Get to bed now," Xiaohai would say. Then the next morning he'd ride me over to the subway station on his bike.

Only once, while we were talking, did the subject of his former girlfriend come up, and he said he ought to have spent more time with her, but he'd been so caught up in practising the guitar that he hadn't found the time. After they broke up, feelings of regret settled in, but . . .

"Do you know how to cherish someone?" he asked, revealing an attitude I'd seldom seen.

The sky had turned a murky yellow. Evening breezes set the green vines outside the window and the scarlet window curtains in motion; they carried with them a wet, humid smell. "There was this line in a book I read once, If you keep on living, you can see each other and say 'I love you,' so we need to keep on living, and living well," I replied.

". . . Actually, the breakup, maybe the only reason was not enough love."

There were times when he unintentionally revealed tender feelings, which I found touching—I say unintentionally, since he was a master of self-control. One autumn day, when we were by Beida's Weiming Lake, he asked me which period I'd pick if I had the choice. I said my childhood. He said he'd choose the present, because otherwise he wouldn't have a chance to know me. Another time he said, "I've discovered a really interesting way to eat instant noodles." He dragged me into his room, where he spread two sheets of newspaper out on the floor and said, "We'll have a picnic."

On many Saturday afternoons, a bunch of us went to his place to play music or just talk, and lots of times we shared our ideals, or went to shows together, and he always looked after me. I was the kid sister who never grew up, always tagging along, forever pure and innocent.

2 9 | I LOVE WUDAOKOU

G and I made a date to go see a concert at The Scream Club in Wudaokou on March 31, the second time I'd seen a show there. After that, The Scream Club changed its name to Oak Club, and became a boring place to hang out. But we had a great time that night. There were so many people you could hardly move, and I spotted lots of kids I knew, including some friends from The Ark and a Japanese friend named Adachi. He pointed to a guy who looked just like him. "That's my older brother, Adachi Takuo."

I told G to hold me when the time came, because I wanted us to look like two people in love. He said he would, but he remained standing there nice and proper. As soon as the show started, though, things really livened up; I was bouncing off people until I was bathed in sweat. I hadn't been this happy in a long time, and people carried me up front and put me down on one of the speakers to rest before I passed out. After a while we went out to get some water, and our ears wouldn't stop buzzing. Adachi treated us, since we'd spent everything we had just to get in to the show.

"That was great." I was sitting on the ground drinking water. I rolled my trouser legs up past my knees, and there was a big bruise on one of my calves. In the light of the streetlamps, I was glad to note that I didn't have thick calves. G looked over at me. "You okay?" he asked.

I was just fine.

All the way home G and I talked about everything under the sun. That's how it always was with us; we'd just say whatever popped into our heads.

We stopped when we got to the Chang'an Shopping Centre, since we lived in opposite directions. Him east, me west.

"Want to sit for a while?" G asked.

"Sure." We walked our bikes over to the parkway in the middle of the street and sat down on a bench.

"Lots of stars out tonight."

"Yeah . . ."

"What are you thinking?" I asked him.

"I was thinking how fucking great it would be to do a show at The Scream Club one day."

"Just keep at it, you'll get there."

"Now what are you thinking?" I asked again as I took his hand in mine and held it gently.

"I . . ." He was about to say something, but stopped. He kissed me lightly. That felt great. After that we sat there talking excitedly, and didn't head home till three or four in the morning, when the sky was starting to turn light.

"Call me when you get home."

"Right," I said with a little laugh. Then I rode home as fast as I could.

30 | BATH

We sneaked into his room. My heart was racing. At first we logged on to the computer and got into a chat room, where we said things like "How come everybody in here's a moron?" Then G played his guitar for a while, until he looked over at me and said, "Let's take a bath."

"Bathe . . . to . . . gether?"

"Why not?" he said. We tiptoed into the bathroom. Standing back-to-back, we took off our clothes, but when we turned around, we didn't dare look at anything but each other's face. The water came in fits and starts. G said that's how it always is in single-storey buildings. After we'd washed a while he gently said, "I'll rub shower gel on you." Stirred by an excitement I'd

the abyss of love river

never felt before, I turned and stared at his skinny, childish body, and we wrapped our arms around each other.

Back on his bed, we whispered as we looked through some comic books. I put on a Cure CD, just the right music for a night filled with fantasies and texture, warm music, making everything just perfect.

We lay back quietly and held hands. He gently kissed me on the eyes and on the lips.

"I think . . . I think I want you. . . ."

"Hm? What did you say? . . . Okay, sure," I said casually.

"I, I want you, you're mine, mine alone." He sounded very determined.

His alone? I'd never consider "belonging" to someone, not to anyone.

So, I told him how I felt about such things, sort of stammering as I did it. He sighed but didn't say anything. He just held me tight.

We set the alarm clock for 4:30. That way we could be out of there before G's folks woke up. By then it was already close to two in the morning.

In the hours before dawn, he quietly caressed my young body: back, innocent face, green hair, feet. Pretending I was still asleep, I lay there without making a sound. It was sheer bliss. By the time we slipped out, early morning Beijing was enshrouded in a thin mist, still asleep.

31 | DESPICABLE, PETTY PERSON

I'm practising love/learning to hold/but too young to know/everything goes

*The name of the game is annihilation/some life ended to begin
Love always ages/Forever is just now.*

The third time we went to his place together, his parents caught us.

At noon on Saturday G had me come to his place to practise. His mother and father were both there. My green hair shocked them, and they asked me how my folks felt about it. I told them I liked my hair that colour. Yang Haitao, his dad, said he was a big fan of music, but popular stuff. G's mother, Xu Juan, said she preferred classical music. First thing every morning, she did singing exercises. According to G, their shared taste in music was what brought them together after their divorces. After practice that day, we left together, and Xu Juan stood in the doorway and watched us. Her gaze stuck to my face like glue, which made me feel sort of creepy and gloomy. She embodied the shrewdness and narrow-mindedness shared by a lot of women who grew up in traditional compounds. I didn't like her the first time I laid eyes on her.

There's a saying that goes, By the time you sense something's wrong, it's already too late. That's how I felt at the time. I sensed that the day would come when she and I would tangle.

One afternoon we were looking for a way to sneak out. G checked several times, but came back each time to tell me his mother was still sitting in the doorway. We didn't know what to do. We even thought about climbing out the window. The minutes passed, and we started to panic.

"G, go buy a newspaper and some steamed buns," his mother shouted from the living room.

I grabbed his hand nervously. "What if she comes in while you're out?"

"No sweat. If she comes in, pick up my guitar and hit her." G smiled to calm me down, but it didn't work. I was still nervous as hell. "You don't think she's sending you on purpose, do you?" I was afraid that while we were trying to come up with a strategy to make our escape, she already knew everything, had already decided what would happen, determined to make things bad for me.

G eased the door closed on his way out. I sat on the edge of the bed reading a book. After several minutes, I heard the door being opened again.

When our eyes met, both our faces went paler than usual. "Just as I thought, there's someone here!" she said with a sneer. "How did you get in?"

I didn't say a word, I just stared at her. Yang Haitao followed her in, took one look at me, and went back to his room.

"Come out into the other room," Xu Juan said.

The blood drained from my face—I must have looked like a corpse. I tried but couldn't say a thing.

At that moment, G came running in. "Your newspaper . . ." The steamed buns fell from his hand and rolled across the floor.

He walked into the room, head down like a good little boy. Yang Haitao walked over and shut the door behind him. "Talk. What have you two been up to?"

G didn't answer. He just stood there.

I glared at him, but he kept staring at the floor, as if he wanted to turn into a statue. He refused to look at me.

"How did you wind up at our house, Jiafu, Lin Jiafu, that is your name, isn't it?"

"Yes." I looked straight into Xu Juan's eyes.

"When did you get here? How come I didn't see you come in? And why didn't you come out while we were eating a while ago? We've always welcomed students, G's classmates, lots of those girls have been here, and if they come at meal-time, they eat with us. If you have nothing to hide, why didn't you come out while we were eating and say hello? Did you spend the night here?

"You know, don't you, that anyone eighteen or younger can sleep over only with their parents' consent?"

I knew that was a new regulation by the Beijing municipal government. The notice had just been published in the *Beijing Evening News*.

She began looking for the copy of the newspaper, and damned if she didn't find it. She held it up in front of me. "Take a good look, it says it right here."

"What sort of relationship do you two have?" Yang Haitao asked from the door.

"I love her," G said.

To both Yang and Xu, this love meant nothing.

"G has been coming home late every day recently, and I know it's because he's been with you! He used to come right home from school, and now he runs around God knows where doing God knows what. Well, not any longer. We'll make yesterday G's responsibility, but that's the last time. If you get into any trouble from now on, don't blame us for the consequences. Write down your parents' phone number, I want to talk to them."

"No!" I said, outraged.

"I'll call the police and report you for trespassing. Now, are you going to give me the number or aren't you?" She picked up the phone. In that second, I knew I hated her.

"No, I'm not."

"Well, then, show us your student ID card." I walked into G's bedroom, picked up my backpack, and handed my ID card to them. They scrutinized it before handing it back.

"All right, then, you'd better go home now. You can come back again, so long as you let us know ahead of time. There's no need for you to go sneaking around."

"Can G walk me part of the way? There are things we have to talk about," I pleaded.

"Yes, but don't be long," Yang Haitao said.

"Come with me first," Xu Juan said. "I have something to say to you."

She led me into her kitchen.

"Girl, how could you be so foolish? How can a boy like G be responsible for anything? What does he know? If something happened, you . . . what good would he be? It's always the males who come out without a scratch. . . ." She grabbed me by the shoulders, "What will you do if you get pregnant? A girl your age can't have the baby. Maybe it wouldn't mean much to you, but just think what your mother would say. Just think."

When we returned to the others, it looked like Yang Haitao had had a talk with G too.

"Can I go now?" I asked them.

"Yes, please do."

G and I walked together out of the family compound. I didn't say anything for a long time. I couldn't figure out why he hadn't done anything to defend me, why we weren't united in our hatred for the enemy.

We came to a roadside bench and sat down.

"It's okay," I tried to comfort G, "it's really okay." He started to cry.

"What's wrong?" I asked.

"Nothing."

We were both feeling cold and sad, as if once I left him today, we'd never see each other again. I asked him what Yang Haitao had said when his mother called me into the kitchen.

"He told me to be careful and not pick up some disease."

He'd fooled me. I'd never thought he could be that cruel.

32 | I HATE YOU BOTH

The pall of what happened at G's house filled our hearts and simply wouldn't leave. And the more I thought about it, the more confused I became. G had acted like a coward, definitely not like a vigorous, spirited young man, a rock music fan who regularly bragged about what a punk he was. How he had behaved was the opposite of what he claimed to be.

I dyed my hair again—red this time. G went with me to Wudaokou to have it done. At first I was planning on dying it pink, but the stylist suggested red instead. He said he'd dyed a guy's hair red a few days before, and it had turned out great. I said I'd give it a try and ended up loving the way it turned out.

* * *

I spent the night at G's place again. I had to. Every time we went to a rock concert, it was over so late there was no place else we could go. At four one morning, we were dressed and ready to leave. No sign of life in Yang Haitao and Xu Juan's room. Then—

"Come in here, G."

We heard the terrifying, drawn-out sound of a woman's voice. G's head sagged, and we exchanged looks. Without a word, he walked out of the room. Then silence. No more than half a minute later, he came back in, this time with his mother. I just looked at the two of them.

My red hair stopped her.

"What's going on, G?" she asked, looking away from me. He kept his head down, like he owed someone money, and held his tongue. Just looking at him made me so mad I couldn't breathe.

"We . . . we have a rehearsal in a little while," G muttered.

"Shut up!" I screamed at him. "I'm going to kill you both! I hate you!" I cursed through clenched teeth and glared at the woman. She was stunned, sort of lightning-struck.

"You hate us for what?"

"You know perfectly well!" I shouted. Brushing past her, I stormed out of the room.

The early morning breezes chilled me. "Dumb cunt!" I cursed as I walked down the street. "You dumb cunt!" G caught up to me and then walked beside me without saying a word. The early sunlight shining down on my red hair was comforting and empowering at the same time.

When we reached the bus stop, he said he'd wait till the bus came. I didn't want to take a bus, I was too damned mad. The way G shied away from standing up to his mother and never questioned her attitude baffled me.

G said he never imagined we'd clash like that.

"There are lots of things you've never imagined," I replied.

*　*　*

My friend Luo Xi surprised me by phoning one day. I recalled that he was a Libra. He had pink hair and a weird way of talking. He was always smiling. Really skinny.

When I answered the phone, a slightly affected male voice said, "Hello, I'm looking for Chun Sue." I recognized the voice at once.

"I know who this is!"

"Who?" I could hear the excitement in the voice.

"Luo Xi!"

"It's me, all right." He laughed. Not a hearty laugh, but a strange, childish one. It was infectious. I laughed too.

One thing led to another, and pretty soon we were talking about his girlfriends. "Have you got one now?" I asked.

"Not at the moment."

"Why not? You just break up?"

"She left, didn't want me, went back to her own country."

"A foreigner?"

"Chinese. Emigrated to Australia."

"Oh. No sweat," I comforted him. "You'll find another."

"I'm in the market for one with red hair." He giggled.

We talked a while longer, some of the time about sex. I asked him questions, and he answered them all.

"Any girl who calls me up and asks questions like that winds up going to bed with me."

"Is that right?"

"People are always calling me up and asking me questions like that . . . and in the end . . . I give them the answer they're looking for."

"Maybe I'm the exception."

He kept hinting over the phone that we were good for each other. Finally I gave in and agreed to meet him, just to talk, outside the Chengxiang Shopping Centre. It was hot and muggy that day; he was already there when I arrived, his once-pink hair now a very light golden colour.

"Hi." I waved.

"You're here."

"Yeah."

"Where do you want to go?"

"Let's just walk," I said.

We drew a lot of attention as we walked, and not just because of our red and gold hair. I ran into someone I knew on the way. She yelled my name. "Jiafu!" But she couldn't believe her eyes when she noticed my red hair. "Jiafu, so this is what you're like these days!"

I could understand her surprise. She was a neighbour woman who had a son my age. We'd gone to primary and middle school together, and she was always telling him to model himself after me, because she thought I was a studious, well-behaved girl. She could hardly believe that I'd actually turned into a "rebel", that her icon had feet of clay.

Luo Xi and I talked off and on as we walked. We had to climb an iron fence to get into the Yuyuantan Park. Then we walked across the lawn to Bayi Lake and sat down on the cement ground around it.

"I'm skinny, aren't I?" he said. "I don't like meat, if I did my skin wouldn't be this fair." He giggled as he scrutinized his skinny arm, then giggled some more when he turned to look at me. I looked down at my deeply tanned arm and gave an embarrassed laugh.

"You are skinny. What do you eat?"

"I don't get out of bed till after noon. Once I'm up I buy a bottle of President Iced Tea and four little éclairs. I guess I eat something later at night. I don't eat much."

"I really like so and so," I said to change the subject.

"Oh, he got into drugs back in ninety-five or ninety-six, and he's been kind of crazy ever since. He used to be on the heavy side, but he's skinny now. And he's not a good guy. He brings a different girl home with him every time."

"So? He's just enjoying himself," I said.

Luo Xi gave me a meaningful look.

The wind off the lake got stronger and colder.

"It's cool here," I said.

"Yeah."

We left the park. I took his hand when we were climbing over the fence. "You don't have to do that," he said.

From there we went to the shopping centre and just hung out in one of the arcades. It was warm, and there were few people, which made it an ideal place to sit and talk.

He started playing around with my address book. He wrote: *Lagwago*

NOFX

punX

SkaCore

* * *

Hardcore

Ska sucks

Maybe I hate you . . . like you, Sex

"I want to have sex with you," he said.

I never expected him to be *that* direct.

"Let's grab a bus to my place. You can spend the night there."

"Doesn't your mother care?"

"Nah. I bring girls home all the time."

"Sounds great. But . . . I can't go." I realized my heart was thumping, but all I could say was "I can't go".

I put my arm around his shoulder. "Don't let it get to you," I said to comfort him. "Maybe some other day."

"No, why can't you make it tonight?" He dropped his head in a pout.

"Not tonight," I repeated, swallowing hard.

"Why?"

"Because, because . . . I love G. I don't want to be with anybody else." It took some effort to say this. "You and I probably aren't right for each other."

"I need to prove to you that I'm better than him."

I really didn't give a damn one way or the other, except that when I thought about how this would affect G, there was nothing more I could say. I suddenly realized that I couldn't recall who all I'd been in love with, their faces were just a blur.

"Actually, I think that the ideal sexual relationship would be like some of those American clubs, like The Sand Club, where everybody's got the same spirit as everyone else, where everyone's free, and they're all sincere on a basic level, including nakedness and open relationships, so long as you don't attack or force your will on others. No holding back, no concealment." I spoke with ease and conviction, like a girl who'd been around. In fact, I had no confidence in what I was saying.

"I have to say there aren't many girls like you. That goes double for China."

What was he saying? I wasn't really listening, I was asking myself why I couldn't do it. I liked him, and he liked me, so why couldn't we? It was all so inconsistent. On the one hand, I was someone who advocated sexual liberation and was opposed to people who tried to monopolize sex, but on the other hand, I was hypocritical in my approach to G and Luo Xi. According to my own logic, I ought to have gone with Luo Xi, jumped into bed, and fucked his brains out—that would have been the right way to do it, the correct way to enjoy life, since I didn't feel that casual sex could have any effect on my emotions.

"Who says we don't have feelings for each other? A girl who likes me, who hugs me, comforts me. . . ." He put his arm around my shoulder. We stubbornly clung to our stances.

"Shall we go?" he said.

Pride meant a lot to him, and I could see that my refusal had injured his self-respect.

34 | A PROMISE

I phoned G and told him what had happened, and he said he wanted to come and see me. We sat on a bench near the Princess Tombs subway station. It looked like it was going to rain, the night air was on the cool side, and G said he was coming down with a cold. I told him I hadn't gone home with Luo Xi because G and I had an agreement. Truth is, I was already starting to regret my promise to G. I didn't want to tie myself down. G didn't understand my logic, felt I didn't appreciate true love. But to me freedom is critical, and it's useless to deny or ignore it. People are born to be free. I didn't know what put that idea in my head, but it was perfectly reasonable to me, even though I couldn't put it into words. I could only describe what restraint felt like.

"When I was young, the sky was pale white, at least that's how I remember it. I'm talking about before I was four, when I was really little, even before I had to go to school. In the afternoon, my parents took naps, leaving me in the next room to play by myself. I hated afternoons like that, oppressive as hell, surrounded by silence, except for the cooing of pigeons, the damp, dank, dark room producing a sense of hopelessness, cold indifference, and monotony. At the time I knew nothing about death, so all I felt was the oppressiveness."

Lots of people were heading in one direction, like the tide, running to catch the last subway. G, his voice betraying a tone of sentimentality, said, "Back then, instant noodles counted as gourmet food, that plus a fifty-cent soft drink."

The ease of his childhood affected me. I put my arms around him. "I won't goof around with anybody else."

He left satisfied.

35 | A COWARD

I went to work as a journalist at a fashion magazine. A brand-new one, just getting ready to put out the first issue, not yet on sale. They came looking for me, saying they liked my writing. The day G accompanied me to the magazine office, I wore a form-fitting green Converse T-shirt and a red miniskirt with a pair of pink Converse sneakers. "You look like a middle school student. See how young our Chun Sue is," the editorial chief, Miss A, said enviously.

The first person I met was an editor named Louise, who was about my age. She came to the regular Monday meeting wearing an elegant pink dress, which heightened the glow of her cheeks, and made her incredibly bewitching. The dress was a bit much for my taste, but it looked great on her, and I guess that meant she had more expensive tastes than I. She was writing a book that would probably be published in a few months.

"You make a cute couple," she said to G and me. "I like you two."

The office was in the Xuanwu District. I didn't have to show up every day, three times a week was all they expected of me.

When G was in school, we talked on the phone at noon-time just about every day, then I waited outside his school in the afternoon, so we could hang out in one of the shopping malls. His class monitor was a chemistry teacher. G said he was a pain.

I didn't like the noisy street his school was on, but I did like the trees and buildings across the street. It seemed refreshingly cool there. At sunset, people were out on the street selling newspapers, their slight accents turning the words "Night paper!" into "My hardcore!" I often tried to ape their accents: "My hardcore!"

It was like a never-ending vacation. During that period, no one told me what to do or what not to do. I could go crazy having fun, and no one cared: I could sing, and I could stay out all night, although the power of tradition lay just below the surface and held me back a bit. I was always struggling against myself.

G had some good news: Xu Juan had moved back to her parents' house. She was afraid. And Yang Haitao asked G if I knew any members of a secret society. He told him I only knew members of rock bands. But that was enough to scare the shit out of them, since rock musicians in those days were little more than hooligans, and you'd be stupid to underestimate them.

One day I told G I'd like to meet his class monitor. He said okay and took me to school with him. Classes were just getting out, and a wave of excited students was coming towards the gate. We were swimming upstream. The classroom building looked pretty old to me, and the hallways were dark, but the feeling I got was a lot better than the vocational high school I'd attended. Normal high schools had a "healthier" student life. G said his class monitor was in his office waiting for him. I was a little nervous when we went in, since it had been a while since I'd been in school at all, let alone a teacher's office.

G's chemistry class monitor was dark and skinny, likely a graduate of one of Beijing's second-rate colleges who stayed in the city to teach high school. He was from a mountain region somewhere. G told me the man was still single, maybe because all the women figured he was next to penniless. He'd turned his office into a dorm room, where he spent most nights. The garish cover of his comforter proved his plight. He seemed confused when one of his students came in with a girl he'd never seen before, but he quickly figured things out: Ah, this must be the girl who spent the night with G and was so difficult for his parents to deal with.

I forget what G, his class monitor, and I talked about that day. All I know is that while we were talking, G and I held hands. During those days, we were really tight, like it's written in books, or shown in movies, or recited in poems, and I experienced the sweet, rich feeling I'd never known in previous relationships. Holding hands was something we had to do, even in his teacher's office. It was beyond our control. We smiled all the time and looked lovingly into each other's eyes.

After a while, he'd seen enough: I am, after all, your teacher, and you ought to have a little decorum in my presence. It wasn't the poor teacher's fault, at least I didn't think so.

* * *

During my extended vacation I decided that I wanted to study German. I didn't choose French or Italian, because I felt that Germany was more remote and stronger than France or Italy. The Rhine flows all the way through it. It's the perfect country for contemplation. But my mother wasn't pleased with my choice; typical of her shortsightedness, she thought the decision to study German was frivolous. I begged and I begged, but she refused to come up with the tuition. After that my self-respect was so damaged that I quit attending continuation and study classes. I wanted my mother to know that studying is a kind of right and not something bestowed from above.

One day G went with me to my former school. My red hair was fading. We squatted by the road in front of the school and smoked cigarettes. School hadn't let out yet, but a few students came out to dump trash. They wore white shirts, black Western pants, and ties. How familiar that was! I watched them with cool detachment, feeling that I'd changed a lot over the past half year or so, but they were exactly the same, hadn't grown up at all. We didn't go in, because I suddenly felt very jaded. I'd gone there to talk with some former classmates, but what I saw made me realize we had nothing to talk about. G and I climbed onto our bikes and rode off. I went home and dyed my hair black.

My mother went over to West X High one day, and when she came home she passed on two pieces of news that made me mad enough to explode. First, I wouldn't be admitted into my senior year; if I wanted to come back to school, I'd have to repeat junior year. The other news was that G's parents had gone to the school, asking after a student named Lin Jiafu: She won't stop pestering our son and she's always spending the night at our place, her hair's green one day and red the next, and what are the school authorities doing about it? When I asked when that had happened, I learned it was right after the first time we were busted by his folks. My face burned when my mother told me this, from embarrassment and from shame. My mother wanted to know what I'd done to offend them, and when. By then I was crying and felt hot all over.

I ran into the bathroom, where I held my head in my hands and wondered how this had happened, how things had turned out like this. My tears came in spurts, I was furious.

Later I phoned G and gave him a quick rundown of what had happened.

"We're over, G! They actually went to school to get even with me! I can't go on like this! Now you go and tell your father and mother that you'll do exactly as they say, because you and I are no longer a couple!" It felt like all the blood was pumping out of my body. Tears gushed from my eyes.

"You're not serious, are you?" came the response after a long pause.

I stared out the window at the green lawn, shadows from all the tall buildings, and the white rays of sunlight, and suddenly felt like I was going to faint.

My mood those days was like dry logs that caught fire and burst into flames for hardly any reason. At the time I was serious about wanting to take a cleaver to those two. I'd never murdered anyone, never even seen anyone get murdered, but I felt I was exhibiting laudable self-restraint. G's passive, deferential attitude only stirred up my anger and anxiety.

Sometimes the phone would ring in the middle of the night, and I would wake up with heart-pounding terror, afraid it was G's parents calling, yes, they're on their way, want to talk to my folks, get everything out in the open. There was nothing I could do about it.

36 | ANOTHER COWARD

Early morning, very cold.

I spotted Louise outside the magazine offices. She seemed elated in her blue-lens shades, and no wonder: She had understanding parents, a rich boyfriend, and the pleasant nonchalance of a typical Libra, with everything going her way.

I don't know why, but I suddenly felt the urge to go back to school, even if that meant repeating my junior year. Maybe I was running away from something. I told my mother I wanted to go back to school. I called just about everyone I knew to tell them I was probably going to resume my studies, and without exception, they said "Great". They also said I should have done it long ago, that I needed to learn new things, or at the very least get my diploma, which would be required if I decided to take exams to continue my studies.

The only person who opposed my plan was G. He said, "What can you learn at that place? Give this plenty of thought before you make up your mind." He knew I hated that school, that I had to think it over carefully.

I even called up my former classmates and told them I planned to come back to school. First was Xie Sini, but she wasn't there, off having a good time somewhere. Chen Xu was at home, and she told me she'd come first in the entrance exam for clerical training. Xie Sini and Cui Xiaodi also passed. Du Yuan was placed in a trade section. "How could she get into clerical training with those grades?" Chen Xu said with disdain.

I waited twenty minutes then dialled Xie Sini's number again. She recognized my voice right off. "Jiafu? . . ."

"It's me," I said. "I'm coming back to school."

"I knew you'd have to."

"Why?" I asked.

"No reason. You're coming back, that's great. Which section?"

"I don't know yet, all I know is I have to repeat junior year."

"Hey, as long as you're back in school, what difference does it make? This way we'll be able to see each other all the time."

I had a dream that night that was all about memory; it seemed as if I'd transferred from school to school but couldn't recall a thing about any of them, except for one person, Xie Sini. She was the sum total of my recollections. I was really losing my mind. I couldn't remember, I couldn't think of anything except for the one person who filled my head, Xie Sini, Xie Sini.

A week before I was to be back in school, I told myself it was time to calm down.

I dug out my gym clothes, my uniform, my tie, a desk cloth, things I'd need at school.

I figured I ought to start getting up at 6:30 every morning again.

The past six months seemed like a dream. Drifting; I hoped I hadn't wasted all that time, I hoped I'd done some of the things I'd always wanted to do.

I thought about what I'd done during that period, what I'd gained and what I'd lost. It seemed like I'd lost a lot and gained hardly anything. I'd dyed my hair, I'd written a few essays, I'd never performed in a show, I hadn't written a novel, I'd been cursed at, I was a lot stronger, I had trouble sleeping, tossing and turning at night, from anger and fear or revenge. I'd become addicted to McDonald's, I'd discovered that a certain brand of clothes fit me nicely, and that my cosmetic supply was still short of mascara and hair conditioner.

Right before I went back to school it drizzled off and on for days. I was out doing interviews, always in unfamiliar places.

I was born without a sense of direction. The last day, I sat at a second-storey window looking out at the trees, at streetcars crawling along, their lights on, and the misty, shadowy human figures. A big bouquet of forget-me-nots and a single drooping rose decorated the table. For some reason, I've never had any luck with cut flowers. I buy them one day and watch them wither the next.

*   *   *

On my first morning back in school, I wore a really baggy uniform—white shirt and required pants—my hair was back to black, dyed of course, and I had on blue sneakers. I figured that no matter where I went or what I was wearing, so long as I had my Converse sneakers, I was at my best. Once again I rode my bike west down Third Ring Road, overwhelmed by my emotions; I'd seldom ridden on this street over the preceding six months, consciously avoiding it and the emotional impact it would have had on me. It was currently undergoing repairs, dust flying.

School, it already seemed so foreign to me, even though I often looked back on it in my dreams. Would everything be the same as before? Just like the first time I walked my bike in through the gate, Director Wang pointed to me and said, "You, there, push your bike to the side. Are you a new student?" When I saw it was Great Old Wang, I nearly stopped breathing, and didn't dare answer him. Hoping he'd think I was new, I obediently did as I was told. I was not considered a well-disciplined student, and the teachers might have already seen my name.

I spotted a couple of my former classmates, Zhang Yan and

Yu Dong, and they gave me a funny look. "Jiafu, are you back in school?" I nodded and gave them a wry smile. "Yep, repeating my junior year." They didn't seem overly surprised by the news, like they knew already. "Well, come over to our class sometime. We're on the third floor of the new building."

Mother and I walked upstairs single file. I looked around, and it was all familiar. Girls in uniforms and ties were sweeping the hallway; I used to be one of them, as if my duty at school wasn't to learn but to work. We walked into the Political Education Office and joined a group of students and parents who were waiting. Director Li was in the centre of the crowd, too busy to notice us for the longest time. "Jiafu," she finally called out, dragging out the sound. Mother and I went up to the short woman, who pulled a long face and said loudly, "I'm very busy today. I don't have time to take care of you two. Come and see me on the second of September, the first day of classes." I walked out of the office and breathed a sigh of relief. At least today I didn't have to stay in school. When all was said and done, the idea of going back was not appealing, but I didn't have a choice. I'd just have to sacrifice today for a better tomorrow.

"Hey there, isn't that Jiafu? Jiafu!" It was two of my former classmates, A and B. They looked really happy to see me. "Hi, Jiafu, are you coming back? Which class are you in? Senior?"

"No," I said, "junior. But I don't know which section. I pity the one that gets me."

* * *

My mother and I returned to West X High at seven in the morning on September 2. Director Li told me I'd been assigned to Junior Section 7. "It's our best class, and I'm putting you there as a special consideration. It's a class for foreign affairs PR secretarial training. You'll have to work hard this semester," she said solemnly, "and no tardiness or absenteeism." All the time she was talking, teachers came in to make work reports. The political instructor, named Jing, told Director Li that the opening ceremony was about to begin. He hadn't changed a bit, and he left without seeing me. I noticed a pile of *Class Monitor Handbooks* stacked in a corner of the office, waiting to be handed out to all the class monitors. A line on the covers read: "Minor Class Monitors—Major Responsibilities". I smiled wryly.

"You are not to fall foul of the school's regulations . . . did you paint your eyebrows?"

"I . . ."

"Wash that off as soon as you leave here, and the next time you do it, it'll cost you points. For now, write me a letter of compliance and fill out a conditional enrolment form. Wait here until I return."

I stood there quietly staring at the enrolment form. It said that the school had the authority to expel any student who violated school regulations. I read carefully, then signed my name—Lin Jiafu. Over the past half year I'd nearly forgotten what my real name was, because "Lin Jiafu" was associated with school, and I'd wanted to distance myself from that place as much as possible so as not to have to think about all the unpleasant things that had happened there. My mother was standing at the window watching the flag go up to signal the beginning of the school year, and listening to the latest "address from beneath the flag". I wondered what was going through her mind. Maybe she was thinking about how kids from other families came to school filled with energy and a positive attitude, while hers had turned out like me. I couldn't know what she'd had to put up with over the past six months, or what she and my father had suffered.

With these thoughts on my mind, I wrote out my guarantee:

> Dear Director Li and School Authorities:
> I promise to obey all school rules and regulations, to study hard, to observe strict discipline, to be punctual and not leave school early, and to complete all graduation requirements. If I fail in any of these, I will abide by the school's disposition of my case.

Director Li returned with a young woman she introduced as the language teacher for Junior 7, Miao Qing, my new class monitor. She wore her hair as short as a boy and had a bean-sprout figure, short and wispy, no match for the slightest breeze; she looked like a kindergarten teacher. Which I later found was exactly what she was cut out for. Miao Qing gazed at me with her big eyes. "You're Lin Jiafu, aren't you? I'm here to welcome you to Junior 7. Why don't you come with me to my office, where we can talk?" Mother and I followed her out of the vice principal's office and over to the vocational high teachers' office, where we were scrutinized by several female teachers.

"Have a seat. Here, try some of this candy." Miao Qing slid two chairs over for Mother and me and held out a bag of mixed candies. She said they were from one of the teachers, who had just gotten married. I knew right off she wanted to get on my good side, but I was a little resistant. "Jiafu, I hear you were enrolled in the first semester of your junior year. Why'd you drop out?" So Director Li hadn't told her why I'd dropped out of school in midyear. Before I had a chance to answer, my mother jumped in: "Oh, it was for health reasons . . . her health."

"And now?"

"I'm fine now," I said.

"Oh." She didn't press the issue.

"Will you be buying the books for this semester?" Miao Qing asked, looking up at Mother.

"I can use my books from last year, can't I?" I said.

"There might be a few changes, so maybe you'd better order a new set," Miao Qing suggested, with a look of concern.

"Well, I guess so, if there might be changes." My mother was clueless, and the school was only too happy to skim a little extra money off one of its students.

Language was my first class, taught by my class monitor.

We went upstairs together, to the third floor. My original classroom. The students stopped what they were doing, and the room went quiet as everyone turned to stare at us.

"I want to introduce you to a new student, Lin Jiafu. She finished a semester of her junior year, where she was a member of Junior 6. Let's all welcome her."

I was met with a round of applause.

I walked to the back of the room and sat down at an empty desk.

Teacher Miao wrote down the semester schedule for our class on the blackboard. It was going to be a dead-on boring semester. We were going to study language, maths, English, politics, finance and accounting (a new class), plus study hall, class meetings, secretarial skills, flower arranging (a new class), computers, Chinese, gym, calligraphy, and our daily technical class. No history no geography no philosophy no music no biology no physics no chemistry.

As soon as the period was over, people swarmed up to ask me why I wasn't in the senior class. I told them it was because I'd originally planned to study abroad, but ran into trouble with my visa application, and that took so much time I had no choice but to repeat my junior year. I also told them how honoured I was to have been assigned to the top section and that I definitely would not do anything to tarnish their reputation, blah-blah-blah. I could see they all believed what they were hearing, even looked like they envied me—I'd already be in a foreign land if my visa application hadn't been rejected. Maybe they were happy because I'd called their class a "top section".

Telling the truth was never part of my plan.

The number of boys was aggravatingly less than the year before, only two in the class. One, named He Yu, was the section leader, the other, Zhao Yinan, was a member of the sports committee. It took several days for me to get the two of them straight. Sitting to my left was a quiet, slightly overweight girl who wore glasses and whose skin was unnaturally pale. In a voice about as loud as a mosquito's buzz, she told me her name was Wang Hui.

Three girls in the class tried immediately to make friends with me. Lively Ji Xueying, Wang Ziqi, who looked like a doll and never had an opinion on anything, and colourless Song

Lei. They were nice enough, but I couldn't help but think that all the kids in this section were inferior to my former classmates, in both looks and brains. Their favourite haunts were the indoor markets Golden Star and Heavenly City, and they never tired of saying things like, "Jiafu, guess how much this backpack cost?"

I'd glance at it. "Fifty?"

With a proud shake of the bag, she'd say, "Wrong. Twenty." Then a few days later, I'd get, "Jiafu, guess how much this pencil box cost?"

I'd look it over. "Twenty?"

With a proud shake of the box, she'd say, "Wrong, five RMB!"

If I then asked, "Where'd you get it?" everyone would be thrilled. It would either be Golden Star, Heavenly City, or Vantone. Some of the more faddish students listened to H.O.T., but none of them read newspapers or magazines. I thought back to my former class, where just about everybody was reading *Modern Music* and *Ruili* . . . it was enough to make you cry. Not to mention Cui Xiaodi, who bought copies of *Southern Weekend* and *Beijing Youth Daily*. How, how did I wind up in a dumb-ass section like this?

At noon I took my lunch box and stood in the cafeteria line with everybody else. Du Yuan, still in uniform, stood in the doorway to monitor discipline. She was now a senior, and I heard one of the junior boys talking about her, saying she was the "school flower". All the girls our age used to say she was loose. As I passed by her, she looked at me and said coolly, "Yo, it's you, Jiafui."

I said, "Hi." She was as eye-pleasing as always, her legs even leaner than before. Her eyebrows were pencilled in thinly, her hair covered half her face.

I sat down at a table with Ji Xueying, Wang Ziqi, and Song Lei to eat my lunch. The other kids also sat down in groups around the cafeteria, except for Wang Hui, who was the only one at her table, head bowed as she ate alone. I asked Ji Xueying why, and she whispered that no one wanted to eat with Wang Hui, that she was a little weird. She seldom talked, Ji Xueying told me with a little giggle.

After lunch, I went downstairs alone to the billboard to see the list of the "three good" students, the group picture of the outstanding class, and a display of vocational skills. There was a photo of Du Yuan with Director Wang and Director Li. She was wearing a spotless white blouse and a smile like a flower in bloom, the picture of youth. The caption beneath the photo said: "Du Yuan, head of the literature and art section of the student club, an active participant in many organized school activities, always for the school's benefit," and so on. When did she become such hot shit?

Two computer classes were scheduled for the afternoon, the subject I always hated most because I was so slow composing characters on the keyboard and because everything was done on a cold piece of machinery. My new teacher wasn't bad, a lot better than Teacher Wang had been. Wang was home on maternity leave, and if she hadn't been, it would have been one hell of an awkward scene to see her. I made up my mind to study really hard.

* * *

37 | IN THE YELLOW SKY

After school that day I spotted a young guy with dyed hair walking down the street, a skateboard slung over his back. I wondered if I knew him, so I slowed down, and when I turned to look, he was looking right at me. He was Japanese, light-skinned with dark lines around his eyes, and in that moment, I wanted to say or do something, though I didn't know what, so I just rode off.

Glass, our drummer, left. Disappeared, vanished to some distant place. In the space between reality and ideals, he chose reality. That was his personality, and maybe he was right, but it wasn't the choice of an idealist. There was nothing wrong with it, he just wasn't an idealist.

The first few days back in school just crawled by; our teachers were crashing bores, stuffy and proper, none of them giving me a single reason to be interested. Miao Qing taught language—murdered it is more like it. In all the language courses I'd taken, ever since I was a kid—thousands of them—I'd never had any this boring! Each class began with a reading of new vocabulary—holding the book out in front as required. In the past, liberal arts teachers had let me do other stuff in their classes, like read a novel, write a journal, stuff like that, since they knew I'd already studied what they were teaching and usually came out on top in tests, and I assumed Miao Qing would see I had a natural talent for language and cut me some slack. So I was surprised when the first time I took out a magazine in class, held it under my desk, and started reading, she kept looking over at me, and finally she said that we should all keep busy with whatever the class was supposed to be doing and not violate classroom discipline . . .

which really pissed me off. From that moment on, I lost all hope for her.

I hadn't been back at school for many days when I discovered there was something funny going on between Miao Qing and the class monitor He Yu. Not only was he her right and left hand, but he seemed to get along with her on a personal level as well. Besides that, the "exceptional class" had so many rules and regulations it made your head swim: Junior 7 never lost a point in the weekly behaviour tally, always ranked number one, an inspiration for all. The kids would rather spend the whole day glued to their desks than lose a single point. He Yu could take most of the credit for this exemplary behaviour. He and Miao Qing were the only two people who had the authority to lead and speak for the class. To say each day in this class was like a year would be an overstatement, but changing "day" to "month" is no exaggeration at all. I started to miss my first year in high school; if back then I'd only been a little more patient . . . but no. Then that wouldn't have been me.

* * *

Back in school I was expected—again—to participate in West X High's once-a-semester, monthlong military training session.

"Starting today, you must be at school by seven-thirty, duty students by seven-ten. We'll drill downstairs."

The news nearly knocked me out.

But I did it anyway, showing up every morning at 7:15 on the button, then going downstairs with the class for the formation drills. I didn't miss a single session, which was a first for me. Director Li ought to have been pleased to see me with an open book in my hands each time she checked on our morning study session. The junior class was her responsibility this semester, and I was probably her biggest headache among all the students, even though I tried hard not to give her any trouble.

To my surprise, Miao Qing still wasn't satisfied. She probably was unaware of my earlier troubles. Either that or she was just incredibly uptight. She didn't like that I got to school at the last minute, even though there was nothing wrong with that, and Junior 7 lost no points because of it. She was in the habit of making oblique accusations—pointing at one thing but cursing another. Everybody in the class knew I was the target, but she never actually named the little slut, the new kid in town.

We weren't allowed to bring outside books to class. And we weren't supposed to rest our heads on our desks during study time. We couldn't write letters. We couldn't read magazines. He Yu would make one sweep of the classroom after another. Absolutely scandalous. A few days in, Miao Qing took me aside to tell me not to wear red, pink, or yellow sneakers, that the school permitted only black, white, blue, or other plain colours. No one had ever said anything about my sneakers before, and pictures of other students in the eye-catching red Korean sneakers they wore every day flashed through my head. But being dumped into a school like this, what could I say?

*　*　*

Wang Hui wrote me a note in class one day:

Let's chat.

You said you were writing up an interview with several bikers, and that reminded me of a middle school classmate of mine who was a motorcycle freak. You said none of them were good-looking, but I think he wasn't bad. He said other people learned about motorcycles on good bikes, but he had to learn on one so old and run-down it almost shook his bones loose. It was hard for him. At one of the student meetings, he demonstrated his skills for us. You've seen so many biker boys do stunts. I'll bet they were spectacular.

Also, I think you've lived a much more fulfilling life than I, you've got your own band. . . . But you're always saying you're bored, that just living in this world is one big bore. That's a gloomy way to look at it. Where this school is concerned, I know you . . . you've got your opinions, and I pretty much agree with you. But there's a lot of fun and interesting things out there, don't you think? Like your band. Away from school, you can be a free person. I agree that this is one boring place, but what can anybody do about that?

I wrote back to her, and we began exchanging notes in class just about every day. One day, Wang Hui took out a brand-new notebook and suggested that we use it for our notes from then on. We started eating lunch together, and she wasn't lonely anymore.

As I see it, everybody's got problems. I study hard because I have to if I'm going to pass the college entrance exam. In today's society, if you haven't got a diploma, nobody wants you. Actually, my mother doesn't want me to take the exam. She and my father are divorced, so there's only her income for the two of us, and college tuition is really high. But she finally said I could give it a try. She's a good mother, and I feel sorry about all my demands on her.

Wang Hui said she and her mother had a good life, a lot better than it used to be, although she'd recently put on weight and couldn't take it off. She said she was a sensitive girl who took everything to heart. She didn't like being quiet all the time, because society took advantage of people who didn't say the things they ought to say.

From my conversations with Wang Hui (we usually didn't exchange more than a few sentences during the day, but communicated regularly on paper), I found out that we were the same age, that as a kid she'd taken time off from school because of an illness serious enough to have to stay in a hospital, that she enjoyed calligraphy, that she was an introvert. I asked her what she thought about our section and about the school in general.

I tried to get into a regular high school, but failed the exam, so they sent me here. I'd like to take some time off, but we've invested too much money for me to do it. I hate this school. And I don't think the kids in our section are as good as my classmates in middle school. Some of them are selfish. There are some good ones, but not many.

Teacher Miao and He Yu got together last year (when he was a sophomore), and I think they're more than just friends. That's what I think about the section, but what can you do?

I dreamed I murdered Xu Juan, in the classroom no less, with witnesses. G was there. I hated her, and was cursing her as I buried my cleaver in her neck. Her head fell to the floor. It was very exciting. I walked up to G. "I've killed her at last, because I hate her so much I'm willing to sacrifice my life to end hers!" I walked back to my desk and looked over at G, who sat down next to me, to my left. He applauded me. The rest of the class joined him. I laughed joyously.

I called G and told him about my dream, not leaving out a thing. He didn't say anything at first, but finally said, "We'll be together forever." It was what he wanted, but just saying it did nothing to dispel my doubts.

That was what I hated about him, that passive attitude. "One of these days you'll understand what I've gone through for us," he said. "Someday things will change, but the people will stay the same." What he's gone through? Him? Unnecessary forbearance and silence?

The first autumn rain fell.

During that first autumn rain I thought about the golden sunlight in my hometown, glinting off the golden grain, the golden fields and golden rape flowers. In my memory my hometown is always golden, always sunlit, always happy. Ever since I was a child I've always longed for that yellow colour that had shone on my body.

I didn't know how to go about finding my lost passion, but my dreams had not been fulfilled, and so I was still young.

38 | CRASHING BOREDOM

Tuesdays were our sports meets. Another boring day, as you can imagine, but fortunately, I could listen to music with my headphones. For the drill competitions we had to be at school by 7:15, and the athletic superstars nearly went crazy. I got to school on time and still got chewed out. After the sports meet, the schedule was changed so that classes started at 7:30. I couldn't figure out why the hell we had to be at school by 7:30, since morning study sessions didn't begin until 7:45.

Our National Day holiday started October 1 and here's how my week went: on the 1st, hung out, had some fun; the 2nd, rehearsal at Tongxian; the 3rd, hung out, walked around Xidan, at night went with a friend to buy speakers; the 4th, a miserable goddamn day, waited for somebody to call or come over, at night went to The Ark, saw Boiled Water . . . the 5th, I forget what I did; the 6th, rehearsal, G was bummed out, so was I; the 7th, went to the magazine office.

I really truly wished I could go back in time. I was about to turn seventeen, getting on in years, and all my passion gone. I thought back fondly to when I was twelve, when I was eleven, when I was just a kid. I didn't know which of them was the real me.

Somebody once asked what I dreamed for the most, and all sorts of crazy things flashed through my mind, money, a good job, travel abroad, fame . . . but what I said was, "I wish I could go back to my childhood."

*   *   *

I had a crazy fucking dream. G and I were standing on the side of Nanlishi Road when a gust of wind blew over our bikes, and a car ran over mine. We shouted curses at the driver, and wouldn't you know it, it was a police car, and we became fugitives from the law. Then one of the young cops fell for me, and I fell for him. Hm, a dream of romance. I also dreamed I went back in time. Back in our home village, I found that my grandparents were a couple of youngsters, and I asked them what day it was. They told me the date. Then I asked them what year it was, and they said it was 1992. I'd turned back the clock! Ecstatic, I ran into the house, where my older brother was sitting on the brick platform bed, him and some other relatives. They were eating dinner. I went over, took my brother's hand, and said, "Finally, I've come back in time, and I'm dreaming about you right this minute. I've turned back the clock!" Deeply moved, my brother started to cry, but we both fought back the tears. When I woke up in the morning, I couldn't tear myself out of bed.

39 | QUITTING SCHOOL FOR GOOD

By winter I wanted to quit school again. I phoned my friend Xiao Shen, and he was very objective about it, not leaning one way or the other. But I really wanted him to give me his honest opinion. G told me I should quit, since I couldn't learn anything there anyway.

It was a really hard decision, and Chinese avoid decisions, even if their life depends on it, since making a decision that determines your fate is a lot harder than simply closing your eyes and waiting for death to take you away.

I figured I had the right to do one of two things: live free or die.

Much to my surprise, a Japanese friend of mine, whose Chinese name was Cui Chenshui, called to say I could stay at his place. This ignited what little hope I had left. My heart was fluttering, partly because of this wonderful yet impractical plan, and partly owing to his kindness and concern. I told Wang Hui I might be quitting school and moving in with a friend, and that if I didn't show up the next day, that meant my plan had worked out. G didn't seem to like the idea that I'd be living so far away, but what were my options? He couldn't help.

First thing Monday morning, I scrambled out of bed, picked out a few clothes and a new pair of green sneakers, and walked out. I was wearing my school uniform and carrying my backpack, which even included that day's textbooks. I changed clothes in a McDonald's bathroom and sprayed on some perfume, but that didn't slow my heartbeat. I looked down at the now useless clothes in my hand, and wondered if I should give them to someone for safekeeping or simply toss them in the trash.

I realized I was incapable of thinking straight, and that depressed me.

* * *

Cui Chenshui was standing to my left, rocking with the motion of the bus, G was standing to my right, with his arm around my waist. The interior lights were off, and light from streetlamps and neon signs illuminated the faces of all the passengers. The outlines of Cui Chenshui's face were hazy.

He was talking about a mutual friend, telling us how great he was, how much he loved his girlfriend, how when he was away on tour he wrote in his diary, "Of all the stars in the sky, you are the brightest. . . ." Cui Chenshui had it memorized, and his hopeless romanticism made me laugh. "What kind of punk are you?" I scolded him.

"I had a girl living at my place not long ago, my god, what a freak she was," he said with his Japanese accent. "She went off the deep end with pills, and for a while, when her boyfriend wasn't around, she had another guy over . . . her boyfriend loved her to distraction, and if he'd known what she was doing, he'd have gone nuts."

Cui took us to his neighbourhood, and his place was a hundred times better than I'd imagined. It had everything, all the comforts of home.

The next morning, Cui and G left at six o'clock, but before he took off, Cui told me there was food in the fridge.

I slept till eight, and couldn't sleep anymore, although I stayed in bed a while longer, feeling bored. When I finally got up, I didn't forget to fold the quilt and smooth out the sheets. Japanese are neat freaks for the most part. The night before, after G and I had showered, Cui spent I don't know how much time alone in the bathroom cleaning up after us. I learned my lesson. I planned to keep his place as neat as a pin while I was living there.

I checked out the kitchen—only instant noodles and some fruit jam. I dumped a package of Chef Kang's noodles into a pot of water and made myself a cup of coffee. When I'd finished my quick meal, I didn't know what to do next.

I turned on the TV and checked out all the stations without

finding anything worth watching. Bummer. I looked down at the ground through the kitchen window; all that whiteness made me light-headed. I thought about going downstairs to walk around, but that didn't sound very appealing, then I thought about calling Cui, but I didn't know what I'd say to him.

The apartment was freezing, the heat hadn't been turned on yet. I couldn't stand the cold, the kind that burrows under your skin little by little. It scared me, made me shrink into myself. I wanted to listen to some music but didn't know how to turn on Cui's stereo, how to turn on his VCR, or how to use the synthesizer. I felt like someone who's been sent into exile, filled with a sense of loss, of mishaps, and of something I couldn't put into words. I began crying bitterly.

I wanted to go home.

G returned around seven that evening. He began griping the minute he stepped in the door. The bus was too crowded, it was a two-hour ride, and he was beat. If not for me, he said, he wouldn't be this tired. . . .

I told G I wanted to go home. "Have you thought this over?" he asked me.

"Yes, I can't hang around this room any longer, I'll go nuts. Nobody to talk to, not a sound anywhere."

"How are you going to make things right with your folks?"

"I don't know. I'll figure that out when I get there," I said.

I left a thank-you note for Cui Chenshui on the dining table, picked up my backpack, and walked out with G. Slight feelings of sadness rose in me as the taxi sped out of the neighbourhood.

I wondered if I could make a living writing.

I opened the door with my key that night and went straight to my room. My parents were asleep, and no one got up to yell at me, the prodigal daughter. I wondered why they didn't at least try to understand my mental complexities. They had no idea how scary, how hopeless my thoughts were.

When morning came, I stayed in bed, greedily soaking up its warmth. No school for me that day, I was thinking. But I knew that lounging around would only drown me in lethargy, take me that much further beyond the point of no return.

"Open the door, Mingming." A burst of rapid knocks at the door brought me out of my reverie. My mother was using my childhood nickname.

"Mingming, open the door, I want to talk to you." The door might as well have weighed a ton. I couldn't face the sombre look in her eyes.

"I'm going over to your school in a little while, so what are your plans? What should I tell them? . . ."

She may have said more than that, but I didn't hear it, maybe as a silent protest. The little bit I heard was enough to just about kill me. I couldn't begin to express the degree of embarrassment and guilt I felt toward the anxious woman standing on the other side of the door. Before I'd thought things through, I'd already made life miserable for others.

"Tell them I'm not going. We can look for a private extension class in a few days."

"But that's short-term. What are your plans for after that?" I detected the sadness hidden deep in her question.

"We'll see when the time comes."

Her footsteps retreated in the distance, the door slammed, and she was gone.

I lay back down and warily looked out the window at the gloomy sky, looming like a hazy face: your typical Beijing winter day. I was reminded of how not a second was wasted in the mornings when I had to go to school, how it was still dark when I got out of bed, a ribbon of blue not appearing in the sky until after second period.

I didn't know when Mother would be coming back. I thought about a kid named Zhang Dongxu who'd written a book that was about to be published. He and I were the same age, both in high school, and he'd already finished a novel. People would buy it and read it, and among those people would be at least one person who really appreciated it.

On the other hand, I'd quit school and left home, only to discover that, as always, I'd wound up with nothing, had reached a dead end. A line from Lu Xun said it all: "There is no greater suffering in life than to awaken from a dream and face a future with no path to tread." How could he write something so heartbreaking . . . if there was no path, I'd just have to create a new one.

41 | ROSE PARK

When I called Zhang Dongxu to ask him about writing, he told me he'd started life as a scribbler only this year, beginning with punk graffiti, which he now thought was pretty stupid. "Long Live Punk: I even sprayed it on our classroom cupboard!"

"You did?" I knew I'd have been expelled if I'd done anything like that. Although I smiled, my hand was frozen, and I wondered why I'd phoned him on such a cold day. There was no intimacy or mutual understanding over the phone—trying to figure out somebody else's life from behind a screen will always leave you helpless and lonely. Bitterly cold, blustery winds blew from the horizon, causing brittle tree branches to snap and crack, and all of a sudden turmoil raged in my head, as I wondered whether or not there was anything out there capable of comforting me.

Night was sneaking up, night that brings terror and darkness, but sometimes traces of safety as well.

I carefully applied some lipstick in the dark, then imagined myself, appreciating how I looked through the eyes of a man, a process I found fascinating, even though I knew that made me a narcissist. Ever since I was little I liked making my face up with Mother's lipstick and rouge, and then staring at myself in the mirror. I loved smearing those magical things on my face, watching as it slowly took on unique qualities. I loved those bright shades and was captivated by the colours of 1970s America, a virtual rainbow, flowing lights, brimming with colours, grotesque and outlandish: green eyeliner, mascara, pink and gold rouge, nail polish with sparkles. I loved and admired them all.

* * *

During the day I phoned a guy I'd heard of named T who worked at Gen X magazine, someone who'd once been a musician and was now a music critic. No reason, just felt like talking to him.

To my surprise, he had a beautiful voice, clear and silky. We talked about music for a while, he asked me which bands

I liked, what I did, stuff like that. He also complimented me on my writing, said he'd seen my story "X X X" in the inaugural issue of a magazine. "I enjoyed reading it, not bad, not bad at all."

"Oh, that was written by another girl, my piece was to the right of it," I corrected him politely.

"Oh? How embarrassing. . . ."

"Don't worry about it."

We talked for another five minutes or so, then, sounding a little anxious, he said, "I'm really sorry, but here we . . . aren't supposed to have long private phone conversations, so why don't you give me your phone number, and I'll call you tonight, how's that?"

T called that night around eight o'clock.

We talked for a while, and boy, could he talk. I kept looking at my watch as it went from eight o'clock to ten o'clock. Just about every time he paused, I glanced at my watch and saw that at least another fifteen minutes had passed. I got the impression he was interested in me.

"Will you be thinking about me? Tomorrow?" A slight stammer and a hint of lonely expectations.

"I expect so," I said. "Let's keep in touch."

A light snow fell. I put on a jacket to go downstairs for the mail. That might have been my only daily contact with the outside world.

42 | I'M YOUR ONLY FRIEND

I looked at my watch when I got out of bed in the morning: it was one minute past eleven. It was strange that I'd been sleeping in so late the past couple of days, and pains in my belly made me cringe. My "friend" was already ten days late, and that scared me. Was it possible I really was in trouble? Frowning, I slipped my feet into fuzzy slippers and shuffled over to the toilet, where, miraculously, I saw some spots of red in my panties.

I needed to talk to someone, anyone. I dialled my friend Mary's number, but no answer. T called off and on, but we never talked for more than five minutes, since he was at the office. "I live with my mother, my father died a long time ago. That's made me strong. I quit school when I was fifteen and went to work in a factory, where I carried ladders, changed lightbulbs, threaded wires, wore work clothes, repaired transformers, and changed fuses. During the day I read Kafka and *Melancholy Flowers Abloom*.

"You're right, I don't understand you, and you don't understand me. I accept the fact that we're incompatible. But I don't care, I still want to see if it works out."

He said he'd call me "Love" from now on, because that's the word that represented his feelings for me, and it also happened to be the name of Courtney Love, someone I liked. I said I'd call him "Mint", as in peppermint.

I hoped Mint would keep his job at the magazine office, since that way he'd be able to phone me every day, at least once in the morning, again before lunch, and sometimes at night. That made me happy; he gave me a sense of security, however pitifully small it may have been. Put people in surroundings they don't like, and they can't help getting depressed; they become desperate for a chance to pour out their feelings. That's something I understand.

* * *

That afternoon I went to Xidan with G. I held his hand. I knew we made a great couple, and even though we had very little money between us, we felt good about ourselves, elated. People on the street gave us friendly looks; maybe when a person sees something she likes, all she can do is wish whoever has it good luck.

We phoned the guitarist Xiaohai to see if he was free that afternoon since we were going to go to Xinjiekou to buy a bass speaker. He said he was leaving soon for the Yidali rehearsal studio, so we agreed to meet there.

I don't know why, but the road from Xidan to Yidali Lane seemed bleak. It was winter, the sunlight was deeply textured, and leaves covered the ground, fallen as if carrying their emotions with them.

We could hear the drums as soon as we reached the head of the lane. They were rehearsing. Xiaohai had cut his long hair, which made him look sort of ordinary, like a typical college student. Maybe that's what he wanted. "Hi, Chun Sue," he greeted me. I thought back to that winter when he'd just passed the college entrance exam, and he and I had gone on an outing to the Forestry University. On a hill there we sang all our favourite songs, and he kept his head down while he strummed the guitar, his long hair covering his eyes and giving him a stubborn, melancholy look. That—the feeling I got then—was the real Xiaohai. I pulled myself back from my memories and smiled. "Xiaohai . . ."

* * *

That Sunday, G and I had a date to go to the book city, and I realized it had been a long time since I'd enjoyed the fresh winter air. At the Book City I bought some fashion magazines, but I couldn't help but think that there were fewer and fewer books in Chinese worth reading.

G wanted to go to a movie at 5:30. He pedalled down the street with me on his bicycle, just as the sun was about to set, and from its position above the mountains it spread an orange glow over the Clock Tower and Ancient Tower, while the Central TV Tower off in the distance looked like it was wrapped in mist. I turned to look, and then laid my head against G's back.

When we got to the theatre I discovered that the movie was *Crouching Tiger, Hidden Dragon*. G bought two green tea lollypops, a new flavour. The sweetness spread all through my nerves.

After the movie, as the audience surged out of the theatre, I felt a weird sense of excitement and anticipation. It was bitter cold. The moon was so big it was almost unreal. And so bright, it was as if it knew we were looking.

* * *

I have two older cousins, Li Bo and Li Guang. They're both in the army. The best way out of a farming village, other than getting into college or getting a real job, is to join the army. That's how my dad got each of us into the city, one step at a time. My cousin Li Guang had a bit of trouble and was in the hospital, costing the family a lot of money, and sometimes my parents complained about him behind his back. But Li Guang and I got along really well. He came into my room, and I told him I was about to leave for the Book City, and that Mother had told me to go with him, since it was on his way. At first I wanted him to drop me off at the subway station, so I could take the subway to the Workers Culture Palace, but I changed my mind in the cab because I wanted to spend some time with him, since we hadn't seen each other for a long time.

We didn't talk in the cab, which sped by the peaked tower of the Armed Forces Museum with McDonald's Golden Arches across the street, past Chang'an Shopping Centre, where the trees had been lush and green, past the billboard at Parkson that's lit up at night to proclaim "Long Live the Fatherland", and past the Clock Tower. Li Guang got out of the cab, paid the driver, and, when I wasn't paying attention, stuffed a hundred-RMB bill in my pocket. I kept the bill. We were always short of money.

I asked the driver, "What do you think, is it better to struggle on your own or to ride on someone else's shoulders?"

The driver said, "Struggle on your own, of course."

"But that takes so much time, and it's a tortuous path."

The driver paused a moment, then said, "However you choose to do it, if you reach your goal, you made the right choice." I'll be fucked, he was right.

*　*　*

Back home I got a phone call from G, who asked where I'd been all afternoon, why I hadn't gotten in touch with him. He sounded panicked, and I felt really bad. I was so selfish, and I hated myself for even thinking about other guys. I didn't want to be unfaithful to G, that's not what I wanted at all. I squatted down on the floor, unable to think of anything except that I loved him and didn't want to lose him. . . .

I thought back fondly to the summer when I'd spent all my

time with G, how I'd ridden over to his school every afternoon to meet him. My hair was red back then, refreshing green trees lined the street. Now all that seemed so far away, the beautiful times when I was sixteen, the excitement of my rebellious years. What did I have to do to return to those beautiful days?

43 | LET YOUTH STOP FOREVER AT SEVENTEEN

Don't speak to me
Hide your eyes

Will it fluster you
If I sit in your lap?
Why would you care?
Are you afraid of me? Do you love me?

Someone once told me
Beauty is ephemeral
But I like to look at fallen leaves
Tell me that I was young once
Tell me I'm still young

I've never seen the sun set behind a mountain
Casting a shadow over the wildwoods
Where raindrops fall
The wind and yesterday are swept away
And I would rather live in dreams

If you meet me today
Will you recognize me?

It was Tuesday, the day I was supposed to meet G. But I was running late, because once I started talking on the phone to Mint I couldn't stop.

On the subway on the way over I was already growing agitated, and my face showed it.

Coming out of the subway station I walked into a headwind that tousled my hair. I saw G sitting on a bench looking at me, a cigarette in his hand. I walked up to him slowly, he tossed his cigarette away, threw his arms around me, and, like an actor in a corny movie or TV soap opera, planted a big kiss on my lips. "I thought maybe you weren't coming." I smiled. "I'll cry if you cheat on me. . . ." He was joking, of course, but there were real tears in his eyes.

"Sorry," I said, "I shouldn't have been late."

As usual, we went to a music and video shop, then to the Converse store to look at their newest sneakers, portable CD players, shades. When we were looking at bathing suits, he turned to me and said, "I'm getting a naughty feeling." I laughed out loud.

I picked out a little green notebook, and G went over and paid for it while I went downstairs to cruise the cosmetic counters. There were lots of things I wanted to buy, some of the newest nail polish by ZA, green eyeliner pencil, perfumed powder, Red Earth white eyeliner pencil, coloured mascara, and L'Oréal liquid foundation, which was cheaper and moister than other brands, so you didn't have to wet your face before you put it on. Then there were Revlon ColorStay lipsticks, since I was tired of using nothing but light colours on my lips; I might as well not use any lipstick at all in that case, and save the money.

I listened to "Say Forever" by Go Go & Me Me on the way home. I'd heard the song by the brother-sister group with the weird names the year before and seen the video on Channel 5, red leaves, pale faces, helpless looks in their eyes, a street with lit streetlamps, a piano, long skirts, and a hobbyhorse rocking in the night—all of which seemed very mournful. Ever since getting the album, I'd listened to it a lot.

* * *

Seventeen years old. I suffer over my inability to write beautiful sentences, suffer over not knowing from experience an exquisitely subtle melancholy, and suffer because I cannot hold on to time, which is so fleeting.

I told G there was a hole in my heart.

He laughed and asked if it could be plugged.

I didn't answer him. I didn't know.

* * *

Afterward, I wanted to say that no one could plug the hole in my heart, that it was lost, that it was lonely.

My seventeenth year slipped away just like that. Day in and day out I sprawled across my desk writing fiction, knowing I had to abandon my today for the sake of my tomorrows. I wanted to change my destiny. My father and mother didn't give a damn about my future or my ideals, all they cared about was whether or not I could get back into school or, failing that, get a decent job. They gave me no money, wouldn't let me make phone calls, I had no decent clothes, no mobile phone—I had to be completely self-reliant. Sometimes I looked up from the pile of books and gazed out the window at the sliver of blue sky beyond the tall buildings and thought to myself, this is the perfect time to be strolling through Xidan, a light mist hanging in the air, children selling flowers, and the streetlights casting pairs of lovers in an enchanting yellow glow.

But I was becoming an entrepreneur, investing in myself and waiting for it to pay off. I wanted a car, a Western-style house. Mint was right when he said, "You're just fooling yourself if you think you don't have to grow up."

44 | DOVE CHOCOLATES

It was November 15, 2000, and Mint was outside Parkson Department Store calling me on the phone to see what kind of chocolate I liked.

"I'll go ask the candy seller which is his most expensive candy, and I'll say, 'I'll take it.'"

Mint grew up in the '80s, and sometimes it shows.

He actually had a very unusual past. He was fifteen when he dropped out of junior college, the equivalent of the junior year in high school, like me. He carried ladders at a factory and often rode his bike for several hours just to buy rock music tapes. He wrote a music review column for *At Your Service Paper* for a year. A long time after that, in a 1998 issue of *Music Life*, I saw his "Fan File", in which he described himself as a fan of Oasis and Blur. Back then I was crazy about the Chinese band Pangu so I just tossed the paper away. He'd said he was seventeen years old and used his real name. Later he did odd music-related jobs for Beijing TV and other places. He spent his eighteenth year playing with a band; they all lived together, so strapped for money they subsisted on two meals of fried rice a day. Eventually he quit the band, seeing no future in being a drummer since "society no longer needed hippies". He freelanced as an editor for a music Web site until it went belly-up like so many others when the economic bubble burst. He said his time at *Gen X* comprised his darkest, least successful period. But by then he'd become the youngest of the "Four Capital City Music Rascals", an "imperial" music reviewer with a bit of a claim to fame.

He seemed like a resourceful opportunist, the sort of "whatever society needs I'll do" individual that I found so typical; but that isn't to say he had no talent. His parents, who had no background in music, couldn't help him and wouldn't have if they could. I envied and admired his capacity to endure hardship and live a frugal life, as well as his ability to gauge people's minds through their words and expressions. I guess you could say that his sensitivity wasn't emotional, but stemmed from an aptitude to observe society, a kind of worldly sensibility.

* * *

The next day, Mint sent the candy over by express courier. It arrived in the afternoon, just after I'd put on my shoes to go running. The large envelope contained three sheets of stationery, two bags of candy, a decal, and a one-inch photo of him.

I was blown away.

I was blown away, and by what? By love or some other bizarre impulse?

I didn't dare apply the decal or eat the candy, afraid that Mint might decide he wanted them back and I'd have to peel the decal off my guitar and go out and buy more candy.

The tiny one-inch photo, mounted on a slip of paper, was overexposed, turning his gaunt face deathly pale, hair hanging low over his forehead, a slight trace of madness in the eyes. It was taken in 1997, and was nothing like I'd imagined. But I couldn't say exactly where it differed. Maybe it was just the way it should be.

A heavy weight settled over my heart after reading his letter, and though I knew that Mint wanted me to call him after the delivery arrived, I needed to be alone, I needed quiet. There was that something pressing down on my heart, nearly taking my breath away. I went downstairs and took off running.

I really didn't dare eat any of that candy. What would I have done to earn it? Mint was a very practical guy who expected a return on his investments. Could I give him what he expected? I had my doubts. Maybe I didn't want to know the answer to my own question.

45 | A LETTER

I discovered a letter addressed to me in the lobby.

With its neat, careful handwriting and the name of my vocational school stamped on it, I already knew who it was from.

She'd answered my letter.

> Jiafu:
> Hi, my dear, I miss you. Are you doing okay? What are you up to these days? You said you were going to move to West

Three Flags, so why didn't you? I guess you applied for time off from school. Didn't you say you didn't want to finish school? So why just take time off? Is it possible you might come back someday?

I remember a dream I had once, the shortest ever, no more than a few seconds. In it you and I went our separate ways, and it seemed strange at the time why I'd have a dream like that, and I simply couldn't believe it. I breathed a sigh of relief when I realized it was only a dream, and who could have predicted that one day it'd actually come true? We barely keep in touch these days, and it's a shame. Everything's about the same as it was in class, except that something's missing.

It's turning cold, so don't forget to dress warmly. This is your favourite season, so maybe the cold doesn't bother you.

That's it for now, here's wishing you a good dream.

Wang Hui (Hui'er)
14/11/2000

I wrote back to ask how she was doing, and told her I'd like to have that notebook where we'd held our conversations during and after class, since I might want to use it when writing my novel. I said she could mail it to me or we could set a time to meet, and I'd go and see her.

46 | BO-RING

Wang Hui wrote back. She surprised me by refusing to return our school conversation notebook.

You said you were going to be an entrepreneur one day, and that means you'll numb your feelings. . . . If you're that *mean to yourself, how would you treat me and your friends? I kept reading your letter for a long time, and I don't think we can be friends anymore. When I've got the time, I'm going to burn that notebook. Do you know what the other kids were saying about you after you left the class?*

I tossed her letter into a drawer, not wanting to explain anything.

47 | BEAUTIFUL AS PEACH AND PLUM BLOSSOMS

I finally changed my hair colour again. Because I had dyed it back to black before, the colour was a little off this time, with red showing through in some places. What I wanted was a pure gold colour, the colour of platinum, Madonna's colour, the platinum of Courtney Love. But the hairdresser said my hair might not be able to handle so many bleach jobs, since I'd bleached it several times already, and this time I might really damage it. She said that a few days earlier, a girl had had to bleach it eight times in her shop to get it completely white. Next time, I thought, that's the colour I want, even if I have to bleach it a dozen times.

Later, while we were at Wudaokou waiting for the bus to go home, soft snowflakes began to fall. "Hey, it's snowing!" I shouted excitedly. It was a beautiful day. A beautiful surface hid countless possibilities.

G didn't like my hair. Which surprised me, since he used to really like how I looked with it dyed. On the bus he called me a "formalist". "What's wrong with black hair?" he said. "Real Gothic."

"Form is content," I said.

To be honest, I didn't know what my parents would think

when they saw my blonde hair, maybe they'd be mad as hell again, and maybe . . . maybe they needed more provocation. I'd dyed it twice before, so this could be the time they'd go ballistic, but I knew that if I kept dyeing it, they'd eventually get used to it.

It turned out just as I'd expected. I slept in till noon the next day but was awakened several times by various noises. I could hear the TV set, people talking. They hadn't seen my new hair colour, and my original plan had been to wait till they went out before leaving my room, but I had to go to the bathroom. I held it as long as I could, then covered my head with a hat and headed through the living room to the bathroom. As I walked past my parents, I noticed they both stared at me for a moment, then looked away. When I'd finished in the bathroom and gone back to my room, my mother knocked on my door. "How come you dyed your hair again?" she asked anxiously. "What makes you think that yellow colour looks good?" Then her gaze shot down to my plucked eyebrows. "And what have you done to your eyebrows? Ai . . ." She pointed a finger at me. "You, you . . ." At a loss for words, she turned and walked out. With total indifference, I looked at myself in the mirror. Beautiful as peach and plum blossoms, frivolous and cheap, just the effect I was looking for, I was quite pleased with my new image. Anyone could have me, but no one could have all of me, and no one would ever truly understand me.

*　*　*

My folks' attitude towards me turned ugly because of my dyed hair. They ignored me most of the time, or glared at me, and I had to wear a hat every time I left the house, even if it was just to go downstairs for the mail. They made it clear they didn't like me talking on the phone, and if someone called while I was in my room, they'd tell the person I wasn't home or they'd just hang up. At ten o'clock they unplugged the phone, so I'd have to go out in the cold if I wanted to make a call. And since I didn't have a phone card, I'd have to memorize the pay phone's number, insert thirty fen and tell the person to call me there. Sheer torture. With snow in the air and ice on the ground, that's how I kept in contact with all my friends.

Writing my novel every day was the only way to escape the realities of my life and hold out even a little hope for myself. But there didn't seem to be any end in sight. . . .

Just thinking about the future depressed me.

48 | GRAFFITI

My friend Mary phoned to tell me she'd seen Li Qi at The Ark Bookshop the week before, and that he was younger than she imagined and sort of petite. I could just picture him, a goddamn pretty-boy poet with a pale face and skinny body, all in black leather, looking like he wants to say something but holding back, which makes you feel good by imagining doing it with him. Mary went up and said to him, "You know Chun Sue, don't you?" Li Qi looked awkward, embarrassed. She said he asked her for my current phone number, and, without even trying to be polite, Mary said, "You know G, don't you? Well, get it from him." With a shocked look, Li Qi said okay. That was the end of their conversation.

* * *

I finally met the writer Zhang Dongxu in the doorway of a Xidan music and video shop. As usual, I was late. He was standing in the cold wind holding a can of spray paint, and he frowned when he saw me. "Sorry!" I said. "I'm notorious for being late. I've got an hour I can spend with you." I looked at my watch, almost seven.

"Where to?" he asked.

"Let's go spray some graffiti." I climbed onto his pink Princess bike, and off we went. The wind was pretty strong, and someone shouted to him along the way, someone I recognized but didn't know well. I hated bumping into people I hardly knew, who always asked where G was. How should I know? I'd say. Their smart-ass attitude and knowing smiles bugged the hell out of me.

We went to a place near his house, where the wall and ground were littered with broken tiles, and where there were some towering maple trees. It was only a few dozen metres from a residential area, so every once in a while a labourer would walk by and give us a strange look—all of which made this a great place for graffiti. He sprayed "Fuck Off" in fancy script on the wall. "Your turn," he said.

I laughed and took the can, excited and a bit nervous, not sure what I wanted to do. "What should I write?" I asked.

"Why not just trace over what I just wrote." So I did. He said that spraying things four times produced the best results. I was starting to get a feel for it, so I sprayed "I HATE YOU!" Zhang Dongxu stood back to admire my handiwork. I walked over to a blank spot on the wall and wrote the characters for Chun Sue. He followed by writing my initials, "C.S." in fancy script underneath. I was starting to get hooked on this graffiti stuff. I sprayed "HOLE" and "I Love Courtney". He said that anybody who saw my "HOLE" might think I tried to write "H.O.T." We used up the entire can before we could write "Sex Pistols", and only got as far as the word "SEX".

"Now where?" I asked him.

"I don't know. Next time let's take our graffiti to Wu-daokou and Sanlitun," he said.

"How about my school? I hate the place, and I guarantee you I'll personally write 'FUCK OFF' on the front of the podium."

* * *

Later on G called to ask if I was seeing other people. "You can't cheat on me," he said. Oh, G, how could I ever cheat on you?

49 | THE PERSON WHO BETRAYED HER IDEAL

When love is true, it enters the bones, lasting till the ocean dries up and rocks begin to crumble, ended only by death. Aren't those who are filled with emotion the ones who kill others?

When love is true, it neither stops nor ends, sometimes it injures not only others, but oneself as well. Mostly it injures oneself.

Gu Long, *Passionate Swordsman Emotionless Sword*

I received a phone call from the entertainment editor of the fashion magazine *Gen X*, who wanted me to keep interviewing underground rock bands, adding that he was pleased with what I'd written for the latest issue, and I agreed to think about his request, even though by then I'd lost interest in underground bands. Entertainment reporting had long since stopped being my aspiration.

I'd developed a habit of sitting in front of the computer at nights, but if my father was home, I couldn't, since the computer was in my younger brother's room, and he had to go to school in the morning. Besides, it seemed unnatural to write private messages in somebody else's room, and not safe. I'd asked many times to move the computer to my room, but they said no, without giving a reason, just no. I was stuck. I needed the computer to write, my brother only used it to play video games—I found it hard to believe they didn't appreciate the difference in needs. The only logical explanation was they didn't give a damn about me, couldn't have cared less. And I couldn't do anything about it. Everything that had happened with them hid out in my brain, a mass of confusion that couldn't be untangled.

* * *

"It'll soon be Christmas," G said sort of dispiritedly.

A display of Christmas trees went up at the Parkson Department Store entrance, the strings of lights flashing on and off, but our glances drifted off towards the backdrop of blue sky beyond the trees and the gradually blurring lights. Christmas, a cold holiday, was actually a favourite of many Chinese, one they may have chosen to observe because it gave them another excuse to go wild. G and I just sat there in front of the trees, deprived of any future we could talk about, and of any excitement, with no further goal to share . . . lonely, empty, that's just how it was.

* * *

Another weekend.

I heard the phone ring from my bed, and if it was for me, it had to be from Mint, since G only called later in the day. Someone answered it in the living room, but then there was nothing. "Is that for me?" I shouted. A moment later: "Telephone!" If I hadn't shouted, whoever answered would have probably said I wasn't home. They'd done it before. I walked out in my PJs, and they were sitting on the sofa watching TV, a few feet from the telephone. No goddamn privacy here. I picked up the phone feeling slightly awkward, and, as I figured, it was Mint, who said he was at Book City, where he'd just bought a copy of Zhang Dongxu's book. "I might make a trip to the Book City this afternoon myself," I said. I'd never actually met him face-to-face.

G called a little later. I asked him what time we were supposed to meet that afternoon, but he said he might have to go to his mother's to get some money, so he couldn't give me a time. His elusive answer made me feel like I was surrounded by greyness. I sighed. I sure didn't want to spend most of the day penned up in the house, because lately I'd done so much writing I was getting dizzy. So I phoned Mary and said I'd meet her in front of Book City.

I was late, again, and as always, Xidan was bustling. "Now which one was Mint?" I asked myself. Was he even there? I had this weird feeling that he was in a dark place while I was out in the light, and that he was laughing at my immaturity and weakness. That impression was followed immediately by the feeling that Mint could be any one of the people around me, though I wouldn't know who.

Book City was packed, and I wondered if all those people really loved reading, or if they'd just come in to get out of the cold. Normally, I try to stay away from vulgar places like Book City, and the minute I walked inside I had the urge to turn around and go right back out. Mary felt exactly the same.

* * *

I paged G again; by then it was three o'clock, and I stood there wide-eyed while time flew by. The weather turned our voices cold and sluggish, and I laughed listlessly. While I waited for G's phone call, my gaze settled on a boy's back. His gorgeous long hair and tight-fitting jeans looked great, but compared to Japanese and Koreans, I prefer the Anglo-American style, especially the way Brits look—clean, fresh, classy.

Suddenly my heart turned incredibly soft and fragile. I really hoped G and I could get back to where we'd been in our relationship. I didn't want wealth or fame, and I thought I could give those up altogether. But for some strange reason, they stuck in my brain and wouldn't go away.

G finally called. "I'm at Chung-you Department Store. When are you coming?" I asked.

"Seven-thirty."

"Why?" I was amazed. "Why so late? I can't wait, sweetheart, come now." I was nearly pleading.

"You're with Mary, aren't you? You can easily kill lots of time shopping."

"Don't you place any value at all on our time together? Time is golden, and if you don't come over now, then just don't come at all."

"Fine."

After hanging up, I stood there like someone who'd lost it. What was going on? I was really bummed out by something I couldn't understand. Like grasping for a straw, I phoned Mint, and told him how bummed out I was, and he said something, but it was all muffled and unclear, like I was hearing him from underwater. Finally, I called G's pager number. Seven-thirty, Chung-you, ground floor, KFC.

The image of the anarchist symbol we'd drawn on the window of the KFC shop on the ground floor of Chung-you was still visible.

While we waited, Mary and I wrote some things in the white spaces of the elevator notice on the first floor. I hadn't brought a pen. I recall saying once: A writer leaving the house without a pen is like a girl leaving the house without clothes. We ended up using an eyebrow pencil. Mary wrote, "Marry me, Pengpeng". Pengpeng was her grade school classmate. I wrote: "Love & Mint". When I finished, a sudden sense of sorrow settled in my heart. "Everything's different."

"Who's different?" Mary asked.

"Me," I said. "It's goddamn ironic. But I regret almost everything, and I'm so sad."

The passion that had once flared up in me had been extinguished, transformed into irony and destruction, and there was nothing I could do about it. I felt as though I'd never again find unspoken, shared feelings. The wind left only me behind. I was walking ahead, but I couldn't stop myself from looking back and shedding silent tears, cherishing the memory of everything that had come before. I was reminded of the song "Looking Back" by Pangu:

I have a bottomless heart
My boat has sprung a leak
My boat is about to sink

What has the power to excite
How many years can we hold on to our youth
I walk ahead
Looking back

G showed up at precisely 7:30. He explained to me that he'd called me that afternoon from his mother's, and had to watch what he said, and that he couldn't come until 7:30 because he'd promised to stop off to buy a CD for a friend.

I didn't say a word, but I forgave him.

* * *

"Why don't you come over this afternoon?" Mint said. It was the first time he'd asked me out, but I'd already agreed to go shopping with G. Even though I knew I was in for another boring day, a complete waste of time, what could I say?

I told him that I had to get off the phone. On any given day, without a doubt, I said "Bye" more than anything else; it was the single most emotional, most utilitarian word in my vocabulary. It could be elegant, decisive, cold, or desperate. When I used it with Mint, it signalled a sort of rejection, a noble attitude, a sort of meaningful end. Maybe I knew that the only time I was in control of the situation was when I said good-bye.

* * *

G called Monday night to see if I could come over, because his parents were out. It was a lovely moonlit Monday night, cool and humid.

How familiar his room was, with the same fresh scent I'd detected on his body for the longest time. How could I bear to lose that? We held each other tightly, two youthful, sleek bodies, and I thought about how I'd missed his body. I could feel the deep emotions in the strength of his embrace, and I felt like shouting: For this body, for this skin, I'd gladly give up everything! God knows I really wanted to spend the night with him, not just an hour or so, just as I yearned for a deep understanding, and not just sex.

Materialism tells us: Material things take precedence over spiritual ones.

Material objects are the foundation.

Form is substance.

I was seventeen by the time I was finally able to understand this. Now I've got it memorized and can use it to satirize or alleviate my own sadness. And yet, while I understand the logic, somehow I can't quite convince myself, because when I'm with G, I'm so happy that with little or no money in my pocket, I still feel incredibly rich.

Should you seize the moment and throw caution to the wind, or rely upon your own strength and the struggle for success, the only success you can take pride in? How can a normal person figure out what's right and what's wrong?

There has to be something in this world more important than truth; there has to be something more important than emotions; more important than money; more important than life itself.

What is that something?

6

a new millennium

Don't stop me from ageing
Because I'm still young
—Qu Yuanxin

Father flung a bowl at me. I loved him, but there was no way we could understand each other.

"So, raising you has caused us nothing but trouble. I swear I'll kill you." A bowl came flying across the room and hit my face. For a moment, it felt like the end of the world. My father, we were kin, we were enemies; I only wished we could have been strangers. "Does anyone have any control over you? I ask you, does anyone have the slightest control over you?" I stood there aloof and unmoved, apathetic and unfeeling, entertaining no thought of resistance, not wanting to react in any way. Everything around me was thoroughly disgusting, useless, and the two people who had brought me into this world would never dream that they were the primary source of my suffering.

Even my youth couldn't help me.

I had to believe that all this was only temporary, that everything would turn out fine in the end, that it'd be okay.

* * *

Mint and I met at last, on Chang'an Avenue. I chose to meet him there because the crowds of well-dressed people and all the lights made the space feel metropolitan. I was hoping that a sense of reality would overcome the unsettled feeling I brought with me. Neither of us was a student any longer, so what purpose was served by trying to engage in some sort of refined pursuit? Cruel or not, I wanted to face reality head-on.

As usual, I was late. The day before our meeting I dyed my hair back to black. Now it looked unnatural, too black, and my eyes, in contrast, after not getting enough sleep for a couple of days, didn't sparkle like they should have. Even worse, I discovered that my overcoat was sort of dirty . . . by the time I'd got myself all dressed, I realized I'd never looked worse.

I phoned him before getting on the subway, and he was with a girl. "The three of us can hang out, and I can introduce you to a new friend." That knocked me out. Introduce me to a new friend? Was he joking? Where does a damned stranger get off wanting to introduce me to a "new" friend?

"No way," I said. "I'm coming to meet you and you alone, I don't have a date with anybody else."

"Okay, okay, I'll tell her to take off, how's that?"

I got on the subway feeling less than enthusiastic. Why couldn't I manage my time better, instead of squandering it on boring, insignificant people? It's just that I'm curious by nature. Ever since I was little I've been obsessively interested in solving riddles, and once I get on the right track, I won't stop until I've analyzed all the possibilities and figured things out. Even if the answer isn't what I'd thought, maybe even the complete opposite, the time spent in the hunt is always well worth it. But maybe it wouldn't be tonight.

The subway arrived too quickly at the Fuxing Gate stop, and I sluggishly disembarked. By then it was 7:40, which meant I was already forty minutes late, but I was probably the least hurried individual in the entire station. I didn't want to leave it; I hated the idea of facing him, and I lacked self-confidence, had the strange, inexplicable feeling of being ignored, of being looked down on. It was not a pleasant feeling. A strong wind greeted me as I exited the subway station. I stopped briefly but knew I had to keep going. The game had started, so it had to play itself out. I sucked in a mouthful of air, so nervous I actually thought I might start crying.

A young man walking towards me looked my way. "Hi, there, I'm Mint. Are you Chun Sue? You've kept me waiting a long time."

"Hi," I said, sizing him up: Not too tall, about five eight, small-boned and skinny-looking, tight jeans, a Converse jacket, New Balance walking shoes, and an oversized mountaineer's backpack that made him look slightly hunchbacked. By comparison, I looked relaxed.

We walked down Chang'an Avenue, heading nowhere in particular into a pretty strong wind. I was tense and excited at the same time, and feeling unpleasantly inhibited. Since we barely knew each other, I talked a lot and laughed loud, though both sounded hollow, really hollow. He was a lot better than I'd imagined, though I didn't much like his face or his eyes. They were dull, lacked purity, like cloudy water, but his jeans looked great on his skinny frame, and his backpack was filled with all kinds of cool things. All in all, he seemed like a cartoon character, but he had unique views on things, a guy who was too smart for his own good. Just my type. On the surface, that is.

During the four hours after Mint and I met, our conversation did not go well. I guess we had trouble communicating. Or maybe the corridor was so brightly lit that nothing could be hidden, that things were in sharp focus. Everything about him was alien to me, except for the silver ring on his finger. He kept moving it around, and I'd read in a book somewhere that this is a subconscious display of emotional discontent. Our conversation was frequently interrupted by incoming phone calls, each of which was met with a sigh of relief as he quickly answered and began speaking to whoever had called.

I recalled that G had asked me to call him before I left to meet this guy, but I hadn't. He probably got home late, after seven, and that's when he called Mint's mobile. Mint handed me the phone, but I looked down and refused to take it until he insisted. The voice on the other end was weak. "Where are you?"

"A corridor."

"At Parkson?"

"No. The seventh floor of a high-rise."

"Why can't you talk at a fast-food restaurant?"

A fast-food restaurant? Maybe in G's mind, talking in a fast-food restaurant was somehow safer.

"I'll call you before I leave," I said.

He hung up.

I shrugged my shoulders.

Given our miserable conversation, I should have said good-bye and left in time to catch the last subway train; that way I'd have left myself a way out and could have explained everything to G. What was wrong with me? Something deep down was shouting its unhappiness and unwillingness, something that was reluctant to lose. I wanted to turn the tide, recapture my self-confidence and my feelings, and my curiosity would not be reined in. I wanted to triumph over him. I couldn't slink home now.

I needed connection, more connection, real-life connection.

* * *

I recall that we found a small hotel that day. Even though he was preoccupied, Mint didn't forget to haggle over the price of the room and got it knocked down from sixty to forty RMB. As we lay on the double bed in the tiny, hot and stuffy room, we discovered we'd forgotten to bring something. So we lay there fully clothed, two people who hadn't even met twenty-four hours earlier. My heart was empty, and I forced everything to the back of my mind, where it fell into nothingness. I was pleased with the results. The next morning at precisely eight o'clock, Mint got out of bed, decisively, no hesitation. He was going to work. No trace of the concern or tenderness I'd imagined. I took the subway home.

He didn't give a damn about me.

* * *

The next day, G went to the magazine office over lunch and left some CDs and books I'd lent him with Miss A, asking her to give them to me. I knew it was over between us. I'd gone too far. Not once had I ever thought about how I'd react on the day I faced the final curtain, whether I'd have anticipated it and mapped out a strategy. And so, when the moment arrived, I reacted passively, totally unprepared. I let G go.

51 | LA LA LA

Mint took me shopping and bought me a pair of yellow shades, plus a very "British" knitted hat, which he clapped on my head with a smile. "Looks great."

A few days later he bought me a red "Miss America" dress. I was reminded of the days with G, when we'd tried to decide whether we wanted to use our money to eat at McDonald's or buy a dress that cost sixty RMB.

After shopping, Mint asked me to go out with him that night, said he wanted me to meet some of his friends.

We saw a not very interesting show at a club, sponsored by a record company to promote new artists. Onstage, a guy kept singing "Because we're young . . ." I forget what followed that line, but it pretty much meant you could get away with anything as long as you were young.

Mint introduced me to his friends: "This is AB, this is ABC, this ABCD, this is ABCDE. . . ."

I said hi to them all. They seemed surprised that Mint could actually have a girlfriend. Hell, *I* was surprised. Later Mint told me he'd once had three conditions for finding a girlfriend: one, never take the initiative; two, spend no money; three, invest no time. In the end, none of the girls liked him either. I was interested in ABCD, who wasn't very tall and was wearing a hooded parka. After talking to him I found he'd worked for *Rock TSGQ*. "I've even read manuscripts you edited!" I told him excitedly, drawing a look from Mint.

I showed his friends some of my writing because of how Mint introduced me: "This is my girlfriend, Chun Sue. She's writing a novel." Maybe the fact that I was writing fiction gave him some credibility.

AB, ABC and ABCDE didn't say anything after they'd read a bit, but ABCD said he liked it a lot. He was impressed by the very first paragraph. I think that was because, like the girl in the novel, he was standing there, rigid, watching a performance he didn't like. There was nothing frivolous or deliberately ambiguous about him. A pure, stand-up guy.

* * *

One weekend Mint and I decided to go to Tianjin to shop for cheap secondhand clothes. The train travelled across a plain where footprints, some deep and some shallow, spread across the snowy landscape. Far off in the distance, we saw virgin snow, trees, and a mountain range. The noonday sun caressed us, like a mother, like a lover. I didn't feel like saying or thinking about anything. We smoked one cigarette after another, and ate preserved plums and beef jerky. We were in a non-smoking car, but no one complained.

"Here, listen to some Yin Wu." Mint handed me his headphones.

To be honest, I didn't care much for Yin Wu; he was too small and too sad. Being small was nothing to be ashamed of, but when a little guy like him sang about things like homesickness, humanity, ideals, and drifting aimlessly through life, it was sort of comical, almost satirical. But maybe that was just me.

After a while, though, it occurred to me that Yin Wu's music was great for train rides, that its mood was perfectly suited for a sense of parting.

"I bought that tape the minute it went up for sale. 'Please Believe' is my favourite. The first time I heard it I cried."

The lyrics went like this:

Don't, don't fall asleep, my friend, for the road ahead is long. Don't, don't lose the hope in your heart, even though we had dreams, broken dreams and wounded hearts and were hurt by the passage of time. Maybe you feel discouraged and hopeless, but I want to say this to you: please believe that not every call goes unanswered, not every loss goes uncompensated, not every star stops reporting the arrival of dawn after a dark night, not every dream willingly breaks its own wings, not every seed finds no soil, and not every song flashes past one's ears without staying in one's heart. Though life continues to wreck our dreams and some losses can never be made up, hope continues its struggle. Please put all this on your shoulder, please put all this on your shoulder.

The banks in Tianjin weren't linked by computer, so we couldn't use our bank cards to get money from the ATMs. Mint was very unlucky. It would take him two or three tries to accomplish something others could manage in one, and things that didn't pose a problem to others would become a headache for him. When we got to the point that we were both famished, Mint suggested going over and sitting at McDonald's for a while. "We can have some coffee there. The Tianjin McDonald's leaves a coffeepot outside, so we can drink free coffee all afternoon, so long as we have cups. And we can ask for sugar and milk." It was a great idea. Sitting in a bright, warm fast-food restaurant drives away any displeasure with the world. And in Tianjin, the McDonald's didn't close until midnight, an hour later than in Beijing.

We spent the rest of the night at an all-night café; by pooling our money, we each had enough to buy a bowl of soybean milk. A cold wind continued to blow outside, but inside the shop was warm as spring. I greeted the next day with last night's makeup on my face, but I was excited and happy. Clear skies and fresh air were always invigorating. Hand in hand, Mint and I strolled around the bazaar, the secondhand market, and the Yishidan Department Store, and were happy even though we had no money. It wasn't easy, but we managed.

I went back to work for the magazine. Miss A had tried every-thing possible to get me to return, since my interviews were pretty good and I was easy to work with.

Everyone at the office was surprised when they learned of my relationship with Mint. They said he looked like a little kid, warm and outgoing, not someone who had a girlfriend. Miss A seemed concerned about me. And me, I hadn't got a handle on the situation myself. Still, I tried to put their minds at ease.

Mint and I agreed to meet at the Hepingmen subway exit every morning at eight so we could take the 25 bus to the office together. Eight o'clock was the set time, but it was often eight-thirty or later when I arrived. Every time I walked out of the exit, I'd see him calmly waiting for me, a smile on his face. Sometimes when we got to the office, we'd listen to *Adore* by Smashing Pumpkins or some other CD on a com-puter as we watched the other editors arriving for work, but more often than not we were late. In that case, we'd listen to the music at noon when all the other editors went downstairs to eat. We left together after work and took the bus to a little café by Liulichang, where we drank soybean milk and ate stewed dishes. I could never get used to drinking soybean milk, but Mint always ordered three big bowls, which he slurped down greedily while it was hot. I just had rice por-ridge. I heard that the café had been in business for over forty years. "I've been eating here since I was a kid. The auntie over there watched me grow up," Mint said, pointing to a woman in her thirties or forties in fresh red lipstick. She looked much younger than her age, a bundle of energy and very friendly. She told us her son also listened to rock music and had also dyed his hair yellow. He was saving up to buy something called an electric guitar. After we ate, Mint would either walk me to the subway station or take me back to his house in a small lane in the Xuanwu District. I hated those lanes. Most of the time Mint's mother wouldn't be home; he said she was busy at work. After his father died, she took care of all the household chores while holding down a job. At home, she'd hurry through dinner and go right to her room to rest. I saw pictures of her when she was young, a real beauty. Sadly, she'd changed a lot and put on weight; her looks were gone completely. The passage of time, hard work, and loneliness age a beautiful woman, and having a son only makes it worse. Her fate was a sort of warning to me.

The door to Mint's room didn't have a lock, which meant he had no personal space, no freedom at home. This was the exact opposite of what I'd expected. Walking into his room, you faced an incredibly garish double bed piled high with pillows, blankets and magazines, mostly *Beijing Youth Weekly* and others published by companies he'd worked for. There was a rank odour like something was rotting, and there were shoes everywhere, under the bed and on the desk, Converse next to New Balance next to Converse next to New Balance. . . . To the right of the bed was a drum set that looked as if it hadn't been touched in years. To the left of the bed was a bookcase filled with papers and cassette tapes. Next to that was another, taller bookcase, stacked high with old books and letters. It was a ridiculous place that looked like it hadn't been cleaned in half a century. On my first visit, I was surprised to find Mint to be so fastidious, so perfect on the surface, yet so utterly shabby and disgusting beneath.

Mint walked me home on many occasions. Sometimes the last bus would be gone and he'd wait for half an hour or an hour in the cold for the first night bus.

Neither of us looked forward to the dusty mornings or the exhausting evenings.

53 | A TOTAL MESS

My curiosity towards Mint started fading fast, and was being replaced by dissatisfaction. My biggest complaint was the lack of a mutual, if unspoken, understanding, which made talking to him exhausting. Day in and day out, he was a bundle of energy, that big, counterfeit Polo backpack over his shoulders and New Balance sneakers on his feet, running around like he was on fire, as if he were the busiest man in the world. What I needed was a kind of quiet and steady love, and I wasn't sure he could give me that.

* * *

On Christmas Eve, Mint and I were walking along Chang'an Avenue.

"Let's put a band together," he said.

"What'll we call it?" I asked.

"Don't know."

"How about Electric Rabbit?"

"Electric Rabbit. Electric Bunny. Wooden Rabbit. Wooden Bunny. I've got it. Let's call our band Wooden Bunny," Mint said.

I was jubilant. What a great sound. The Wooden Bunny Band. I kept repeating the name. "Oh! Wooden Bunny!"

"Welcome, everyone. We're the Wooden Bunny Band. For our first number, we'd like to play 'Wooden Bunny'." Mint played air guitar. "OK, our next song is 'Bunny'!" He waved his arms and danced around a bit. "Our third song, 'Rabbit'!" We burst out laughing, completely carried away.

The movie we were going to see had already been running for twenty minutes when we got to the theatre. The tickets were pretty steep, and Mint hesitated for about five minutes. I just looked at him, not saying a word, but I was thinking, "It'll be all over between us if he doesn't just go on and buy the tickets or if he tries a bunch of excuses not to."

"I guess I'm stuck," he said as he took the money out. We ran inside excitedly, groping our way in the dark to find seats up front. I saw people eating popcorn and wanted some, so I told Mint. He said he'd get some during intermission. Talking to him was a chore, because I had to repeat myself ten times. We were having trouble communicating in general, but I didn't want to complain. The first movie was a domestic film that was already half over, so we just soaked up the atmosphere of the theatre instead of watching. The second was a hugely popular suspense film of 2000, steeped in a gloomy, eerie feeling with superb settings: a slaughterhouse and underground steam pipes, a pier, railroad tracks . . . I was immediately hooked.

We didn't know where to go after the movie let out. It was five in the morning and we were tired, but we didn't have the money to rent a room. Neither of us could take the other home because we both had old-fashioned, traditional parents.

"I'm cold," I said to Mint. "What'll we do? Where can we go? We can't just stand here."

"Why don't we go to my house? I'll say to mother, 'This is my co-worker and we have to go to work together later this morning.' You can sleep on the sofa. What do you say?"

"OK."

We waited in the cold wind for the first bus of the day that could take us to Mint's house. He and his mother crowded into the bed in his room, and I slept on the living room sofa. Before lying down, I had to clear off newspapers and other junk. Mint tossed me a filthy blanket with a floral cover, and I covered myself and fell asleep. Later, I sensed that someone was standing in front of me, but I was so tired I couldn't keep my eyes open; I guessed it must have been his mother. It was past eight when Mint woke me up. His mother gave him twenty RMB for us to have jellied bean curd and fried liver at a snack shop. Then we hurried to the office, where we punched our time cards and sprawled on the desks to snooze before the others showed up for work.

54 | BOHEMIAN RHAPSODY

I should pluck a handful of wild grass and walk on silently, feeling neither tired nor sad. My mind is devoid of concerns, I've forgotten all about worldly matters.

Like a weed in the autumn, swaying only because of an occasional breeze, neither happy nor sad. After the wind dies down, the grass remains lush and green, withering in the evening at dusk.

—Ziyu

Mint went with me to watch an alternative girls' band rehearse. They were in the process of reorganizing and wanted me to be their bass. They didn't have much technique to speak of, but they got to perform a lot and were well received. Neither they nor I wanted to admit that gender was the reason they were better received than their music deserved. Mint took the bus there with me, because once again neither of us had any money. I knew he'd be hungry, so I brought some instant noodles along. It was snowing; the ground was cold and hard.

Most of the girls in the band were still in high school. I'd read their lyrics, and some of the words sounded strangely familiar. I suspected they were the Beijing version of songs by a famous foreign lyricist. The drummer, Huang Manman, had dyed her hair yellow. Her favorite word was "fuck", which she said all the time. The lead singer showed me a pair of new shoes made from purple snakeskin, with pointed toes. While we rehearsed, Mint sprawled on a stool and quietly read a children's book we'd bought a few days earlier. It was my ideal book, because each time we opened it, we discovered something we hadn't seen the previous time. So in a way, it wasn't an easy book; after each read you found you had or possessed anew the signs of imagination.

A guy arrived a while later and volunteered to teach Huang Manman to play the guitar. They were giving each other flirtatious looks and joking around the whole time. Whenever Huang Manman played the wrong note, she'd say, "You didn't teach me that!"

"It wasn't that I didn't teach you, it was I didn't pinch you."

"Fuck . . ."

We took a bus home after the rehearsal. The girls took the same bus, because they said they were going to Xidan to buy shoes. I walked with Huang Manman and we chatted along the way. She brought up G, saying he wasn't good-looking and didn't know how to dress. I cut her off and told her no one says anything bad about G in front of me. I felt my heart begin to ache.

* * *

I dreamed about school again.

In my dream, dressed in a white skirt, I was anxiously talking to the senior class monitor and the principal, "Please, I beg you. Please let me attend the senior class." They were unmoved, and I was about to cry like an abused child. Needing to talk but unable to, my breathing was fast and shallow, my voice growing hoarse. I was scared I might die from this desperate struggle. After I got up in the morning, it was all I could do to rid my mind of any memories of school.

On my way to the bathroom, I walked past the big mirror in the living room, and my face flickered briefly before my eyes. "I didn't used to look like that," I thought.

I lay back in bed, as countless illusions flooded my mind, all from the past: a hasty smile; a mood in still frame; the wind, catkins, sun, and the humidity of summer. They came together to form patchy points of light, impossible to grasp.

I'd rather forsake all my memories and turn my mind into a white, sweet nothingness. White would give me a sense of tranquillity and security, smoothing and nourishing every vein, until everything appeared gilded.

* * *

"What we lack is a joining of the hearts. All the time we've been together, my happiest moments have been the times we talked on the phone," Mint said to me.

That hit me like a bolt of lightning. He'd just said what I'd wanted to say. It was true, he could see right through me, like I was a clear stream. Why did he love me? In his eyes, I had all kinds of shortcomings: I was selfish, weak, and immature. So why did he love me? Why didn't he find someone more suitable?

"I don't understand myself. Do you understand me?"

"Outsiders often see things more clearly. Just like you sometimes see shortcomings in me that I don't even know exist."

I was speechless. Was it that simple?

He was still talking, but I don't think I heard anything.

Love? What's love? I could neither answer nor deal with the question. A joining of the hearts? What a joke. I could have died laughing. I'd thought about that question every day, and here he was, asking it. I wasn't a hired escort, and he was no moneybags, so there must have been a purpose for our being together. What was it? Since it wasn't physical, was it emotional? I was such a hypocrite I didn't even know what I was thinking, so how could I give anyone a sober yet emotional relationship? That was my question, my conundrum.

A few days later I got a call from Mint. "I was just thinking about calling you," I said.

There was a lot of static in the background.

I took a deep breath. "I have something to say to you."

"Hey, speak up. There's something wrong with this phone."

"Call me from your mobile phone." I turned adamant. "I'll only take ten minutes."

"Huh?" He laughed. "No way. I haven't paid this month's phone bill yet, and I can't go over the limit. Do you have any idea how much ten minutes costs?"

Before he had a chance to finish, I hung up and unplugged the phone.

I ran into Mint on the 25 bus the next day on my way to work. He sat in front of and across from me, separated by ten or fifteen feet. We stared at each other. After about five minutes he came over. "Why'd you hang up on me yesterday?" he asked. I didn't answer.

I was sure I'd loved Mint. I just wasn't sure if Mint had ever truly loved me. I'm certain his motives for hooking up with me weren't good ones. Maybe he just fell out of love with me. He'd call out the names of other girls while we were making love, he never stopped flirting or caressing, he quickly found causes and excuses for all his flaws: obstinacy, indifference, affectation, and anger. He had an empty goal and hollow gazes, even as he gave his body to me, the vampire. I learned more and grew clearer as we moved ahead, but my discoveries shocked me, scared me, sent my blood racing. I decided I needed to move on.

I didn't tell him what I was thinking. There was already so much he didn't know, and I was determined to see this game through to the finish.

55 | DYING OF TROUBLE

I chatted up a guy in the art section on the second floor of the magazine office. He told me his name was Lulu, and that he was the lead singer in a band. He was an assistant photographer at Gen X. We talked for a while and agreed to take in a show together sometime.

Mint said he knew Lulu too, that they were pals. Every time Lulu paged me, Mint wanted to go with me to see him. He told me not to fall for Lulu. A few days later, Lulu asked me to see a show with him. Mint cancelled an appointment so he could go along. When Lulu strutted into KFC to meet me, he was proudly sporting a mohawk. People gaped at him, but he was unflappable, like someone who was used to incredulous or contemptuous looks. I watched happily, admiringly. Mint was no match for Lulu; he looked mean and fatigued. Lulu ordered a meal for himself and bought me an orange drink. I couldn't help but feel happy.

While he ate, Lulu told me he'd fallen out of love and wanted his next girlfriend to be tall. "At least five six," he said, as he looked at me. I worked on my soft drink calmly, but something began to stir inside me.

"Set me up with someone," he said.

"I can't. I know more guys than girls." Suddenly I thought of Mary. Hadn't she said she was having problems with her boyfriend? "Same old same old," she always replied lazily when I asked her how things were going with him. She had a wild streak and an eagerness to try anything, which I liked. Maybe she and Lulu might hit it off. It couldn't hurt to try, and was a good way to get to know more people. It might even help her with her poetry. Besides, I could tell that Lulu would be good in bed.

"Wait, let me introduce you to my friend Mary. She's nineteen, a college student."

"How tall is she?" Lulu blurted out. The way I figured it, his shitty question was simply an excuse to turn me down.

"I'd say five five."

"Too short," he said.

He could see I wasn't very tall either. Not much more than five five, but I was skinny and had a quick mind. Maybe that appealed to him.

"You know, I'd really like to go to this show," he said, but Mint and I both had our own thoughts about the evening. I wanted to go to Lulu's place; Mint was in a hurry to get out of there.

"I'll go with you next time, Lulu."

"Right. We can all go together," Mint cut in.

We ended up going to Lulu's house. He had a typical happy, middle-class, intellectual family. Both his parents were teachers. They lived in a small neighbourhood surrounded by artists. When he first shaved his head, the only question his parents asked was, "Aren't you cold?" They bought him a computer and a guitar, let him draw on his wall, go online, talk forever on the phone, brought him steamy hot food when he was hungry, and let him bring anyone home to sleep over, boy or girl.

As soon as we walked in the door, a cute little puppy ran up and circled our legs. "Come here, Snowball," Lulu called to him. I was playing with the puppy when Lulu's parents came out to greet us. His father had greying hair and looked like a scholarly, refined old gentleman. Lulu said he taught classical Chinese. His mother, an ordinary woman with a friendly smile, had the grace and ease of a cultured lady only somewhat past her prime.

"Oh, it's Lulu's friends. Come in, please. It must be cold outside."

It was, I thought, as I turned to Lulu's father. "Uncle, I'll come to you with my questions about literature." The old gentleman laughed and said, "You flatter me." Mint's face took on a sour look.

Lulu's room, as expected, was clean and cozy, so typical of a Libra. Sometimes you can tell a lot about someone's personality and how they live from minor details—like whether or not there's dirt under their fingernails. Lulu turned on his computer and said to Mint, "I'll play you some of our songs." Mint knew a lot more about these things than we did. I knew next to nothing about computer software or electronic music editing.

My attention was drawn to the decorations on the wall. Naturally, there were lots of rock posters, like KORN. A gigantic, abstract painting of a human face hanging near the bed appeared to be Lulu's own work. There were also photo collages, and on a picture of himself, he'd written, "Look, this is the courageous Lulu." In each of the photos, Lulu's hair was cut in a Mohawk, long or short, and he generously displayed his muscles, his anger, his beauty. My heartbeat quickened; I liked what I saw, but couldn't tell anyone.

Snowball ran over and plopped down by my feet. I picked him up and held him in my arms, while Lulu played his own music on his guitar. He used Fruit II, a music software I'd never heard of, but Mint was talking a blue streak about it, insisting that Lulu needed to buy some new equipment. I played with the chain on my waist and gave Mary a call.

"Mary? This is Chun Sue." I lowered my voice and walked over to sit on Lulu's bed. "Guess where I am? Do you know Lulu, the lead singer of XX Band?" Not surprisingly Mary knew all about the band. She even said Lulu had sexy legs.

I laughed, but I was bored to tears. The two guys were talking about music and about the future, as if I weren't even there. "My boyfriend is having a wonderful chat with a guy I'm interested in, and they're enjoying their conversation so much they seem to have forgotten my existence. In the forty minutes since we stepped into this room, the only thing anyone said to me was an absentminded inquiry from Mint about how I was doing. Of course I'm doing fine. What else could I be doing? Now they're talking about electronic music and I don't understand a word." I couldn't mask the hurt and dejection. "What should I do, Mary? I've fallen behind the times." I was sure I'd lowered my voice enough, but Mint shot me a strange puzzled look. Five minutes later he walked over, pointed to his watch, and said, "We should be going pretty soon."

With a blank look on my face, I put on my coat and picked

up my backpack. As I was leaving, Lulu said, "Here, have some perfume." He handed me a small aluminum bottle. I opened it. It smelled a little like soap. Probably men's cologne. "For me?" He smiled and said, "I don't use it, except to spray on Snowball sometimes." That tickled me. After Lulu saw us to the door, Mint and I groped our way down the dark hallway and walked to the bus stop. It was still snowing.

"What's the matter with you? I can see you're pissed," Mint said provocatively.

"Nothing."

"Oh? Do you honestly believe that I can't tell what you're thinking? You're upset because I ignored you, right? But what was I supposed to do? I know a lot about electronic music, and it just happened to come up today, when Lulu asked me to listen to their music, so I gave him my opinion. It would have been rude not to, especially since we're all friends.

"And how could you accept cologne from him? Even you said it wasn't very good stuff, that it smells like soap. Other people don't act that way. . . . I'll tell you what it is . . . it's taking whatever you want from people. How can you be like that? It's not like I can't give you things, but you go get them from someone else, and I don't understand.

"Also, what were you saying when we were in the car on the way to Lulu's house? He said he admired me and considered me his idol, and you said, Impossible. You know what, people around me like me, some even worship me. And that other thing you said, something about me exploiting Chinese rock music. I was just . . . I don't know what to say." His eyes reddened, and he looked so mistreated that when he tried to continue he had to pause. "I've never exploited Chinese rock! What should I do when my closest friend says something like that about me, when even she can't understand me?" He went on and on, to the point that he felt sorry for himself. Sitting there listening, I could sense snickers from people around us and felt ashamed to be sitting next to him. It almost made me want to puke watching him rant and rave and expose just how narrow-minded he was.

Finally, we got off the bus. He continued blabbering about things that didn't concern me, and I wondered how long he could keep it up. We found the RBR café by Sogo Department Store, where I spent my last ten RMB for a peanut butter sandwich. Then I took a piece of paper and scribbled something while Mint looked on quizzically. I handed him the paper when I was done, and said, "I'm going to the bathroom."

When I returned a few minutes later, he was still reading what I'd written. After a few seconds he said, "I haven't finished yet, but judging from what I've read so far, it appears that you want to break up." I looked down to avoid him. He reached out to take my hand. "Look at me, Chun Sue," he said urgently. "What's wrong? Are you angry? I admit I was wrong, okay? I went a little overboard." I avoided looking at him, kept my head down because I was afraid I might laugh if I looked up. It was all so funny. I cared a great deal about his views and attitude towards me, but I didn't like him one bit. "Chun Sue." He gripped my hand, "Don't do this, okay? I was wrong. I . . . was too self-centred." He lowered his head and reproached himself with what appeared to be sincerity. But I was totally unmoved.

"I love you, Chun Sue. I don't want to lose you. You and my mother are all I have. I can't lose you. Won't you look at me?" I started walking away, not saying a word. He stopped me and nearly shouted, "Chun Sue!" Then he leaned on my shoulder and began to sob bitterly. I was totally unaffected. "I can't let you leave. You might never come back. You haven't seen it, but there's a movie that shows how sometimes a very minor incident can change a person's whole life. I can't lose you. If you leave today, I know I'll regret it and my heart will ache. I've never said anything like this before, because I absolutely hate the way people say they'll be together forever but really can't do it. But right now I have to tell you that I want to be with you forever."

He held me tightly, his hot tears on my face and body. I just stood there, slightly lost, unable to feel the bone-crushing pain one might expect. Had I experienced that sort of pain at any time in the past? Was it possible that I was thinking about someone else? I could smell the cologne Lulu had given me, and that made the situation even more disconcerting and awkward. I couldn't help but feel that the person saying this to me shouldn't have been Mint.

"I've always worked hard. I wouldn't even give my career up for my own mother, unless she was critically ill, and then I'd stay home and take care of her. But if you want, I'll give up everything for you."

"The most important thing is work." Coolly and softly, I echoed this favourite phrase of his.

"That's not true. Chun Sue, the most important thing isn't work."

My heart was like stagnant water, perfectly calm. It had all come down to this. I was just numb.

I reached out to dry his tears. "Don't cry, please don't cry,"

I muttered over and over. Large snowflakes fell from the sky.

I knew I needed to make myself look hurt, and Mint was surprised to see the dampness on my cheeks, obviously thought I was moved. "Forgive me just this once, okay?"

I didn't believe we could ever communicate, and this somehow seemed incredibly funny to me. But I wanted to avoid an awkward confrontation.

"Let's find an all-night café and talk some more," he said.

I was already exhausted so what the hell?

We walked from Xidan all the way to a franchise of the Yonghe Soybean Milk Shop behind Tiananmen. We stayed there till 5:30 in the morning, then said good-bye.

56 | GET BY JUST LIKE THAT

I know not what they mean/Tears from the depth of some divine despair/Rise in the heart, and gather to the eyes,/In looking on the happy autumn-fields,/And thinking of the days that are no more.

—Alfred Lord Tennyson

G and I saw each other only two more times. The first I asked him to go with me to Henderson Centre to buy some perfume. The next time we went out to eat together. I've forgotten what excuse I used to get him out, but he came. We sat at a table, across from one another, and I felt such a tinge of sadness when I realized that he wasn't mine anymore. Oh my God. Halfway through the meal, a girl paged him and he went outside to return her call. Fifteen minutes later he returned to say a girl would be coming in a while. I wasn't very happy about that. When the girl arrived, she was wearing a black Marilyn Manson T-shirt. We chatted a while. She liked rock music and gave a detailed account of some foreign bands that were hot in China at the moment. I quickly let down my guard. Then she mentioned the singer Zhao Ping and said he'd mentioned me to her once. He said I was a very good person, that he'd fallen for me when we read a story I wrote about a cricket. The cricket died at the end of the story, and he was immediately smitten.

I had written a children's story like that, when I was a freshman in high school. We were in bed when I read it to him, expressively, my grief beyond description. I knew I'd been writing about myself, youth and warm blood flowing away unnoticed.

* * *

.What was the point of love if everything turned out like this? What was the value of youth and beauty if everything was so boring, so dull? What was so special about spring and so different about life if everything was nothing more than what I was experiencing? Don't tell me this is what life is all about. If it is, if I have to live like this day after day from now on, how will my longing heart continue to beat?

I wasn't a mature woman to begin with, so how could I understand the heart of a mature woman? I'd never had one.

Ever since I was a little girl, I've believed that I wasn't an ordinary child. I imagined I was the most beautiful, the most intelligent, and the most talented girl in our village. I knew that one day I'd leave the village, and I wanted to do everything better than everyone else; I wanted to have what I felt I deserved. A love without passion wasn't my kind of love.

I now loathed that innocent me. I despised that unsophisticated me. I hated those innocent years. Innocence was bullshit! Innocence was nothing and could never be anything. I felt so pressured. I hadn't done anything and didn't know how to do anything. What about my future? My tomorrow? Who'd care? I didn't want to go on like this any longer. I wanted to learn English, I wanted to practise my guitar, I wanted to form a band, I wanted to write poetry. I wanted to die, I wanted to die, I want to die.

I received a belated card with only one line—Merry Christmas. The century had abandoned me, no longer certain of innocence, eternity, or happiness.

A whole century had passed. Everything was gone and would never return.

I couldn't recall anything that had come before. My heart was calm and I decided to give it all up. There was no discernible difference between the second just passed and the second yet to come.

translator's acknowledgments

Several people contributed to the completion of this translation. Thanks to Leon Ge, Jonathan Noble, Zhang Xin, Chun Sue's agent in Asia, Edmund Cheung, and Alex Morris, our terrific editor. Special thanks to Kaiser Kuo, whose knowledge of the Beijing scene is encyclopedic and whose generosity in sharing it went well beyond all expectations, and to Li-chun, whose comments on the translation and overall support were, as always, invaluable.